AFFLICTION
2

ASSA
RAYMOND
BAKER

GOOD 2 GO PUBLISHING

AFFLICTION 2
Written by Assa Raymond Baker
Cover Design: Davida Baldwin Odd Ball Designs
Typesetter: Mychea
ISBN: 978-1-947340-45-9
Copyright © 2020 Good2Go Publishing
Published 2020 by Good2Go Publishing
7311 W. Glass Lane • Laveen, AZ 85339
www.good2gopublishing.com
https://twitter.com/good2gobooks
G2G@good2gopublishing.com
www.facebook.com/good2gopublishing
www.instagram.com/good2gopublishing

PROLOGUE

This was now the second day that Promise had gone without hearing Fame's voice. She did get a text, though, in the middle of the night, that read, "I'm good. We're good. Just working." This confused her because normally he would say things like, "I love you," or, "I miss you," or at least respond to something she had texted to him.

"Bitch! I know you're not still running around here pouting!"

"Shut up! Shut your ass up, Endure. I'm not in the mood for your shit right now! I just wish that Fame would give me a chance to explain things about

Drew."

"Maybe it has nothing to do with Drew. Maybe Mr. Perfect is using this time to spend with his real wife and kids that he ain't told you about."

"Fuck . . . you! I know he is not married. His ass might gotta lil punk bitch stashed somewhere, but I'm positive he ain't married. Wait a fuckin' minute. . . Is this your way of telling me Sharky's secret?"

"My man ain't got no secrets! The only bitches his dick is going up in are the ones I choose for us. Mines picks up every time I call and checks in with me all through the day," said Endure, who just received a text from Shay. "Shay wants us to go out with her tonight. She wanna know if you wanna go clubbing or to the Pot. Which one?"

"Nah. . . I'm good. . . Y'all go," Promiss declined. Then she received and read a text from Drew. He was asking her out with him for a friendly date. "Drew just don't give up, do he?"

"Promiss, I'm not gonna let you just sit around here by your damn self like some cat lady. Come out with us, and since Drew wanna be your friend so bad. . . Tell him to meet us at the Pot so we can help keep things friendly while y'all talk."

"I don't need Fame seeing me with Drew again. We haven't talked about who he is yet. So I ain't going to do no clubbing."

"So the Pot it is then," Endure said, and then quickly sent Shay a text back letting her know that they wanted to go to the casino with her.

"Okay. . . Fuck it, I'ma go with y'all, but I gotta go home and find me something to wear."

"I'm not stupid, Promiss. I got something in my closet that will fit ya. I know if you go home, we're not gonna hear from you no more tonight. So. . . Nope. . . Let's go in here and get ready," Endure said, pulling her into the bedroom so they could get dressed to go gambling at Potawatomi Casino.

CHAPTER 1

Fame wasn't a jealous man, only a very cautious one, with some real trust issues. That's why he had rounded the block and parked up the street from Promiss's house after her. There was an unknown man with her. From what Fame could tell, Promiss wasn't trying to give the guy the time of day, but then she hugged him before getting into the van. That was what was on his mind, but he couldn't allow it to fester in his brain because he and Slim had a job to do, and it was a very personal one. The morning after he picked him up to put the Porsche back in storage, Slim's grandmother called and told him that she needed him to come over right away.

Once they arrived at Slim's grandmother's house, she was there waiting, along with his auntie and her best friend, who was also like an aunt to him. All the women were teary-eyed when Slim asked them what was wrong. They told him that his cousin Heather and her best friend Lisa were being held hostage by a pimp who called himself Mercy Bonds.

Mercy Bonds was forcing the girls to prostitute for him while at the same time demanding that their mothers pay him $10,000 in order to get them back. The mothers didn't want to get the police involved and risk him killing the girls, so they paid him what he asked for. He took the ten grand and then demanded another ten grand for the other girl as well.

He wouldn't release either of them until the money was received and said the teen girls would die if he didn't receive it soon. That's when they decided to call Slim, because they knew he had connections that may help to get the girls back.

Fame and Slim left and immediately took to the streets. They cruised throughout the city of Madison looking for any signs of the girls or their new pimp. The two exasperated hit men had just turned into the parking lot of a hole-in-the-wall strip club when Slim received a call from his auntie.

"Is they okay? I know he's there now."

"Bro, did they find them?" Fame promptly stopped talking when Slim held up his hand. Fame, now from the side of the cell phone, could hear that one of the girls had somehow gotten a phone and called home.

"Okay, tell her to look out of the window and give you the address to whatever's across the street from them; then text it to me with as much info on the place as she could see. I'm on my way." Slim ended the call. "They're in Racine. Someplace in an apartment building somewhere off of Main Street," he explained just as the text with the info he asked them for came through.

"We got an address!"

With that said, Fame stormed the Buick through the city and back onto the highway. They rode while wordlessly trying to keep their emotions in check. They couldn't afford for anything to go wrong for the girls or themselves because they were too distracted

with anger. This was kind of hard for Fame to do with

Promiss constantly texting him asking him to call her

and apologizing for Drew showing up the way he

had. Fame did his best to ignore the phone, knowing

it wasn't the time to be having that conversation.

Hours later, Fame parked in front of the address

that Slim's auntie had texted along with a picture of

what was outside the girls' location's window.

"Which one you thinking we should try first?"

Slim asked, red with anger as they sat staring at two

side-by-side apartment buildings that had a few

flashy cars parked out front.

"Let's snatch that lil bitch right there up and see

if she knows him or has seen something that could

help us."

"Nawl, bro, we can't snatch her up. If we scare her, she won't tell us shit. Watch my back. I'ma go act like I'm lost," Fame told him before getting out of the car and approaching the woman who looked more and more like a hoe the closer he got. Just when he was about to speak, he heard her say the name of the pimp they were there for into her Bluetooth earpiece, and he fell back to the Buick.

"What happened?"

"That's one of the nigga's bitches. I heard her talking to him on the phone."

"Why didn't you get her?"

"Bro, ain't shit change for us. This is a job just like all of the others we go on. So relax. We know we're in the right spot and we know what she looks like. All we gotta do is wait for her to go back in the building and follow her to the apartment," Fame explained, trying his best to help Slim focus.

A short time later and the women reentered the building with them following loosely behind her. They caught sight of her as she went inside of the apartment midway down the third-floor hallway.

"Let's go get 'em. We kicking that door in," was all that was said before Fame slammed his foot two hard times on the apartment door.

It opened with a bang, sending pieces of wood and locks flying as they rushed in, guns first. Two other women in the room screamed and dove to the floor as Fame shot a guy who went for a gun lying on the cluttered makeshift table.

"Where the fuck is Heather and Lisa?" Slim demanded, holding a second man by the throat with his gun pressed to his eye. "Lisa! Heather!" Slim yelled without giving the guy time to answer.

"I don't know who you're fuckin' talking about! You got the wrong place!" he exclaimed in terror.

"They're in the back room," one of the females spoke up.

"At least that's the names of the girls back there."

"I'm on it." Fame ran to the door, ramming his way inside, where he found the two dirty bruised-faced teens huddled in the far corner of the room. "I got 'em, bro! They're good!"

"Which one of these bitch motherfuckers is

Mercy?" Slim questioned the room.

"He not here. On my life, Mercy's not here!" said the man he was holding at gunpoint.

"I wasn't talking to you!" Slim whacked him a few quick hard times in the head with the gun.

"Mercy is in Milwaukee. He lives there somewhere. Y'all killed his cousin right there. Please don't kill us! We just wanna go home!" the girl they followed inside pleaded.

As soon as Fame emerged from the room with Slim's cousins in tow, Slim squeezed the trigger putting a bullet straight through the head of the man he was holding. Then he demanded the phone from the girl they had followed inside.

"All y'all get the fuck outta here and keep y'all's

mouths shut because we can find you just like we found them," Fame warned the women. Then the four of them rushed out of the building, hopped in the Buick, and then headed home. "Slim . . . Man, you good? Call big mama and let her know we got 'em"

"I'm good . . . But this ain't over yet! I want the punk Mercy's blood for this shit!"

CHAPTER 2

Even though Mister came out alright from being shot in the robbery, that didn't change the fact that Sharky and Zay wanted the ones behind it. So this made Sharky's hours away from home longer and longer, and left Endure with mixed feelings. She was happy and sad at the same time. Happy, because Sharky had lightened up on her a little, giving her more time to hang out with her girls, which she used to do before they got serious. Sad, because most of the time she didn't get to see him until just before she had to go to work.

Since it was a work night and the end of the month, Endure knew she would have been at home alone had Shay not called for her and Promiss to go out with her.

"Why is it so dead here tonight?" Promiss asked, expressing that she didn't want to be there by using a dull, depressed tone.

"It's still early, Promiss. Stop acting like that. Let's get drunk and try to win more money than we lose. It's ladies' night, a.k.a. Wild Wednesday, so let's have some fun," Shay said while dragging Promiss by the hand over to the first blackjack table they came to.

"This looks like a good place to start the fire," Endure said.

"P, I was just about to go looking for you. I was hoping you didn't stand me up," Drew said suddenly beside them.

"Now, I wouldn't do that to you. But I don't wanna play, so let's go find someplace in here to sit and get drunk before I start giving away all my money," Promiss told him.

Mimi stepped in front of Drew, stopping him from following Promiss, and made sure he knew that they were not to leave the casino without letting one of them know because they came together and they planned on leaving together.

"Hey. I'm just here to have fun, and y'all here to have fun, only I hope to win my girl back and some cash. Not make shit harder on myself," he told her as Promiss took his hand and pulled him away from her nosey cousins and sister.

After Promiss and Drew went off to the bar area, Endure, Shay, and Mimi turned their attention to the game table. Sharky had given Endure petty cash to do with what she wanted, that morning before he went in to work. Shay followed her as she removed a stack of bills of her own. The players at the table closely observed them as they counted out six hundred dollars each to start with and laid it on the table.

The dealer scooped up the money, then spread it out on the table so they could recount it.

"Twelve hundred playing?"

"Yep," they said in unison.

"Would you like this in black chips, ladies?"

"Yeah, give us the big-boy black chips!" Mimi answered excitedly while getting into the game.

"Okay. This is the hundred-dollar table, meaning that the minimum bet is one hundred dollars," the dealer explained as he counted out twelve black chips and then pushed them in front of the giddy trio.

"Mimi, since you ain't ever played this game, you place the bet," Endure said.

"Yeah, bet however many you feel good about," Shay added.

"Ah, man . . . I don't know." Mimi picked up four chips then checked to see if it was too much by looking at the others. When no one said anything, she tossed them in the circle with the other bets.

The dealer began dealing the cards and then flipped over his own. Shay showed them the eleven they had been dealt.

"Hit!" Endure said.

"Four of hearts. Fifteen is showing," said the dealer.

"Hit us again!"

"Two of spades. Showing seventeen!"

"Fuck it! Hit!"

"Four of hearts. Twenty-one," the dealer said with all smiles.

After three more wins, the girls finally lost one, but Mimi had only bet three chips, so the loss didn't put a dent in the stack of chips that was sitting in front of them. Not wanting to press their luck at the table anymore, they went off in search of Promiss and Drew and found them playing the ten cent slots and looking like a happy couple. They decided to let them be and went off to the big Wheel of Fortune game to play.

~ ~ ~

Danny Boy, Eshy, Freebandz, and Boony were also in the casino trying to get lucky. Danny Boy was there to show that he didn't have any hard feelings for almost going to prison because of them. The case

16

against him was promptly dismissed when his lawyer produced video of Freebandz entering and leaving the night club. Danny Boy also got Summer to tell the court that she was the one driving his car that night, since none of what the ADA had actually showed Freebandz getting in the car.

"Say, y'all tripping. I'm finna try to catch me one of these pieces that's up in here tonight, while you niggas over there givin' up all y'all cash," Boony said, eyeing Mimi from across the room. "I think I got me one, and she got a bad bitch with her. DB, come with so you can keep her buddy busy."

"Y'all gon' get your pimp on. I think I got something that's gonna be some for sure money in my pocket," Eshy exclaimed, then pulled Freebandz over to where a sexy little white girl was having all the luck. "Fam, I'm about to go over to the slots so I can keep an eye on that bitch."

"Alright, my nigga! Which ones, so I'll know where to find you when it's time to move."

"Them nickel joints over there," Eshy answered, pointing toward a bank of machines. "I'll text you if I move around from there. But you can believe I got my good eye on the snow bunny."

"For sure, family. I'ma try to get some of my loot back right here," Freebandz replied before he then rolled the dice he was holding.

"Winner!" Eshy heard the dealer call out to him. He knew that meant his luck was now looking better and better. He smiled at his partner as he made his way to the slots.

Boony and Danny Boy turned up the swagger as they approached the Wheel of Fortune machine where Shay , Endure, and Mimi were having a little debate about the cost to play the game.

"Damn, here y'all go. We've been walking around here all night trying to find y'all," Boony said, stopping in front of Mimi.

"Excuse you. Why are y'all looking for us?" Shay questioned, knowing that they didn't work for Potawatomi by the way they were dressed.

"I don't know about him, but I'm just trying to get lucky with you," Danny Boy told Shay as he slapped a fifty-dollar bill down on the game in front of her.

"I'm sorry, but we aren't here looking for you. We're just trying to have a nice girls' night out," Mimi told them.

"Speak for yourself, Mimi. I'm fixin'a see what this fifty gon' make me right here, then see how lucky he really is."

"Shay, you need fuckin' help. I swear I'ma put your ass in one of them impulsive disorder classes and have them ban you from everything for a year," Endure cranked out on them, then walked off reading a text from Sharky.

"Sexy, come rub some of that good luck you having off on me," Boony said to Mimi, taking a seat beside her at the game.

Mimi started to refuse with a smart-mouth remark, but his swagger was overpowering and he was looking good under the hypnotic colorful casino lighting, so she gave in. Endure walked over toward Promiss and Drew at the roulette wheel.

"It's past your curfew," the text said.

"Not if you're not at home. Are you?" Endure replied.

"In bed wising you was here to do something

with this hard dick I'm holdin. So get home!"

"I can't, I rode with Promiss, so you gotta come get me. I'm still at the Pot."

"Did you come up or lose all my money?"

"It's our money, nigga. Get it right. And I ain't tellin' you. LOL."

"It's like that? I'm on my way."

"K," she replied, and then went and informed her sister that she was leaving.

"Bitch! How you gon' drag me out here then ditch me?" Promiss asked, feeling the shots of Patrón that she and Drew had been throwing back since they broke off from them.

"Man, you know how it is. I gotta get it when I can cuz it ain't no telling how long it's gonna be before he takes some more time out for me."

"What's going on? Don't tell me you bitches

about to leave me too?" Mimi asked, suddenly appearing.

"Daddy just told Endure to get her ass home so he can spank that. Where's Shay?" Promiss asked, watching Drew excuse himself from the three of them to talk on the phone.

"Her ass ditched me for ole boy, and his guy took off on me after he got a text from his bitch, I guess. Now this. Which one of you gotta give me a ride home?"

"I'm still chillin' with Drew, so you can take my car since you're ready to call it a night." Promiss handed Mimi her keys. "Don't tear my car up, Mimi. And it better have gas in it when you pick me up in the morning," she warned her cousin.

~ ~ ~

Fame got out of the Buick and followed his

partner into the fancy and busy casino. They had gotten word that Mercy Bondz could be at Potawatomi because he was a notorious gambler.

"I found him!" Slim announced. "Look over at the craps table."

At the same time Fame looked in Mercy Bondz's direction, he spotted Promiss hanging all over Drew. She was just having the time of her life at the packed roulette table.

"Slim, there goes Promiss and that dude I told you about at the wheel right there." Fame pointed. "So let's fall back. It's way too open in here to get Bondz anyway, and there's no tellin' when he gon' get up to go to the bathroom. Let's just wait for him to come out and follow him to the crib," he suggested, which was the best way for them to get their target. But he just didn't want to be in there looking at Promiss with another man.

"Yeah, you're right. That way I can get my granny her money back and our pay for this shit. That bitch-ass nigga ain't gon' need it in hell," Slim said, promptly turning around and heading back out to the car.

About an hour or so later, Fame witnessed as Endure left the casino and got in the truck with her man Sharky, followed by Promiss, the guy she was with, and another girl that Fame remembered from a photo at Promiss's house. Promiss and the girl hugged and parted ways as the valet pulled up to them in an Audi, which was the car of the guy she was with. Right then Mercy Bondz exited the casino with an Angie Stone-looking woman on his arm.

"It's game time!" Slim said, perking up in the driver's seat.

"Yep, I see 'em," Fame said, tightening his grip on his gun as he watched both the Audi and the Cadillac pull away.

Fame didn't have a doubt in his mind now that Promiss was playing him. He shook it off and focused on the task at hand after telling himself that he was done with her. The guy was lucky he didn't kill him for coming around and messing up his life.

Mercy Bondz pulled over in front of a modest upper-southside home and remained in his car making out like a teenager with the woman he was with. Suddenly Slim smashed the window on the passenger side as Fame fired a bullet into Mercy's hip, letting him know not to move.

"Argh!" Mercy Bondz screamed in pain. "You can have it all; just please, don't hurt my wife," he pled while holding her and applying pressure to his bullet wound.

"This your bitch, huh?" Slim hit her with a hard backhand to the side of the face. "I thought your punk ass only liked young hoes."

Fame reached in and pulled the driver door open and demanded all of the cash that Mercy Bondz had on him right then, because he didn't trust going inside of the house.

"Here. Take it and go. That's over fifteen Gs, and y'all can have this truck too. Just let us go."

"Nawl. I don't want your truck. I just want you to know how it feels to have someone you love taken from you," Slim barked, and then shot his wife in the face, killing her, right in front of him. "That's for taking my lil cousins."

Fame quickly pumped two shots into Mercy Bondz's chest and then fled right after because he thought he could see someone peeking out of the next-door neighbor's window when they were actually being watched from inside of the house that they were in front of.

CHAPTER 3

Promiss and Drew sat in her family room talking about their night at the casino and just remembering the special moments they had had together.

"Mimi can't ever do that again. That was a once-in-a-lifetime moment."

"Hell yeah it was. She actually did that by accident!"

"Drew, you know how cheap that girl is? There's no way Mimi would have played that 'play all' button when she was damn near five hundred in the bank. I seen it in her face when she did it, and I didn't

know what the fuck had happened when that screen

went blank. Then, BAM! Jackpot!"

When the laughter died down, the low intimate

lights combined with being tipsy had Promiss feeling

a little warm.

"Do you love me?" Drew asked, moving closer.

"Drew, I told you that I'm happy."

"That's not what I asked you. Do you still love

me, Promiss?"

"Yes. I can't lie. I do and I might always,

Andrew, but I'm just not 'in love' with you anymore.

I was really hurt when you vanished the way you did.

All that pain and depression is why I lost the baby."

"Wait . . . What baby, Promiss? Why you didn't

tell me about a baby?"

"I wasn't sure how to tell you, and I don't know why I just said it now." Promiss had tears falling from her eyes. "You know how much I want to be a wife and mother, and you took that from me."

"I didn't. I was in jail fighting to get home to you. You're all I thought about. As soon as I got out and got my shit together, I came back to you." He leaned in and kissed her soft lips.

Promiss gave in to her lust, kissing him back.

"No, wait! We can't do this, Drew." She pushed him away.

"Let me have you. Let me love you just for tonight. I need this, and I think you do, too, so we can truly move on or not."

Drew pulled her onto his lap and she let him. "Be mine, if only for this moment," he whispered, then removed her shirt.

Promiss was lost in the heat of the moment. Having Drew's lips on hers and his hands on her skin had her so moist and so hot, but her heart belonged to Fame, and that's whose arms she knew she really wanted to be in.

"Drew, no. I can't do this. And if you love me, you will respect this. Please." She stood up trying to catch her breath.

"I know." He shook his head in disappointment. "I'm gonna leave. I pressured you and I'm sorry. I just needed to know that we were really over," he said as he made is way to the door. "Ole boy lucky.

Promiss, all you gotta do is call me and I'm on my way, always." Drew kissed her on the cheek and then walked out to his car.

Promiss fell back against the door after she locked it. Then she picked up her phone and looked at the photo she took of Fame standing, shirtless, at the foot of her bed. Then she sent him a text saying that she loved him and to call her as soon as he could. Then she called her sister.

"Endure, you gotta hold things down by yourself today. I been up all night, and I can't do it," she told her, marching toward her bedroom.

"Did you and Drew?"

"No. Hell, nawl. We just sat up and talked. That's all."

"Uh-huh. Talked. So that's why you ain't been to sleep yet. Cuz y'all was talking," Endure pressed and teased her.

"What I gotta lie to you for? What I do with my pussy is my business. If I wanna give it up . . . I'll do it," she said while lying undressed on her bed.

"And Fame will tap that ass when he finds out."

"Nawl. That's you and Sharky. Just call me if you need me."

"Hey, turn on 58. They got breaking news about a home invasion," Promiss explained, turning up the forty-inch television that was hanging on a wall in her bedroom. The news showed a bunch of police cars and people and a forensic van inside the yellow taped-off block.

"Promiss, that's that white girl that was at the Pot. I remember her there."

"That's why she looked so familiar to me. Didn't she hit like back-to-back jackpots or something?" she added, now standing naked beside her big king-size bed.

"Yeah, I think I heard somebody say she won like almost a hundred Gs. I bet that's why she got killed too."

"Sis, let me call and see if Mimi's ass is okay cuz a lotta muthafuckas seen her win that jackpot too."

"I just texted her, but she called me when she got home."

"She called me too. I gave her my car, remember, but if they ran up in that white girl's crib and she lives in the hood, they'll run up in Mimi's out there in Brown Deer."

"She just hit back and said she's asleep and for us broke bitches to make an appointment when we wanna talk to her." Endure laughed and responded to her cousin's text. "Whaat! Awe, man, that's messed up! I was just with her. Tell Zay that Penny gon' be in my prayers."

"Endure? Endure, what you talking about?" Promiss asked, being nosey while listening to her sister talking to Sharky in the background.

"Sharky just said he knows that white girl that got killed. He said her name is Penny."

"Tell him I'm sorry to hear that. I'ma let you go so y'all can talk. I might be in to work at noon if you can't make it. Have Shay go in and call me," Promiss

instructed before ending the call. She stared at the

photo on the screen of her and Fame until she fell

asleep.

~ ~ ~

Homicide detective Brett Sadd arrived on the

scene way late and a bit tipsy, so before he went in

search of his latest partner, he stopped and conferred

with a few uniformed officers first with hopes they

could bring him up to speed on the double homicide

scene.

"I was in the area when the shots fired call came

in an hour or so ago. So I was first on the scene.

When I turned onto the block, I spotted the SUV with

its window broken and went over for a closer look.

That's when I found the two vics DOA and called it in," the Asian officer explained.

"Has anyone identified the bodies yet?"

"I haven't, but your partner may have. She's all business. Put me right to work on the crowd control as soon as she arrived. She asked me to send you her way when you got here. Heads up, Buddy, she's pissed, and you may want to find a stick of gum or something before you catch up with her."

"Yeah, thanks," Sadd said, walking over toward his partner. Detective Tonya Kare is an athletically built, Emily Blunt look-alike in her early thirties. From the way she was dragging her feet, Sadd knew she had not gotten any rest from their previous murder case.

"You're late!" she barked.

"Hey, I got here as fast as I felt I needed to be here," he shot back at her, not liking what he heard in her tone.

Detective Sadd reminded most people of the actor Jack Black when they saw him. Sadd had been an MPD detective for two months shy of fifteen years and was ready for a change.

"I made a pitstop at the station to try to catch you there, and to my bad luck you had fuckin' gotten called out already," he lied. The truth was that he was on a date with his favorite whore.

"What the fuck do you have a phone for if you never read your text messages? I sent you three telling you about this call and that I was out already."

"I said I was sorry. Now will you please just fill me in on what we got there and save all of the complaining for your hubby?" He flipped open a small notepad and prepared to write down what she told him she had found out about the crime scene.

"Fuck you!" She frowned while storming off toward the SUV.

"Really, Tonya, are you being serious right now?" he asked while staying in step right behind her. Kare stopped in her tracks and took a calming breath before addressing Sadd again. They had only been partners going on four months, and she, so far, hated working with him.

"You missed two dead bodies, one male and the other female. Both were shot while sitting inside the

Caddy over there. They're believed to have been married and both lived there." Kare pointed to the house that uniformed officers were walking in and out of across the street from where they stood.

"Wait. What did you say the vics' names were?" Sadd asked with his blue eyes focused on the Cadillac Escalade sitting on twinkling gold-tipped chrome twenty-six-inch rims.

"Markee Bondz and Felisha Lee Bondz," she answered without having to review her notes.

"Mercy fucking Bondz! I knew that Caddy from someone," Detective Sadd exclaimed. "So he got his ticket punched. The old piece of shit!"

"I said Markee, not Mercy."

"Yeah, I'm thinking they are one in the same

because that fancy whore sled over there belongs to

Mercy Bondz."

"Okay, good, you know one of the vics, so that

should make my job a little bit easier." Kare took out

her pen and pad. "Tell me everything you can

remember about him."

"Well, one of our vics was a pimp that went by

the name of Mercy Bondz. I know the Feds have

been trying to bust him on human trafficking charges

for about a year now. I know he has a son I believe

we need to locate and get off the streets if we don't

wanna be picking up any more bodies off the ground

anytime soon."

CHAPTER 4

For many of the girls, new talent Wednesdays at the popular strip club, Silks, was a slow night, but not for a mesmerizing brick house like Forever. She knew how to work the stage and twerk with such precision that it made it hard for men to keep it in their pants. After her last dance of the night she headed to the dressing room, zigzagging her way through the maze of tables. Forever received even more tips as men tried to convince her to give them a lap dance or leave with them.

"Is everything okay, girlie?" she asked Summer,

who was standing outside of her dressing room leaving an angry voicemail for Freebandz.

"Free's ass is not answering the damn phone. He should've been here to get me by now," Summer explained, now watching Forever removing the crumpled cash that men had stuffed in her tight G-string and garter belt during her dance. "His ass better be in jail, cuz I'ma kill him if he not," she vented as she dropped her phone in her purse. "Can you do me a favor and drop me off at home? I don't trust these cab services these days. There's been way too much going on."

"Yeah, sure. I can do that. But we gonna have to swing by my house first so I can let my puppy out," Forever told her while admiring Summer's long shimmering legs that were coming from extra tight cutoff blue jeans.

"That's fine. I'm on your time. Free probably ain't at home anyways," she agreed, following Forever on into the dressing room so she could get changed into her street clothes.

The two of them had been dancing together at the club for almost two years. They even sometimes performed a girl-on-girl act that all started one night when three new girls didn't show up for work. The club owner asked Forever if she could fill in the open slots for them. That's when she pitched the girl-on-girl idea to Summer. Forever was surprised when she agreed right away, and that left Forever wondering if she could get Summer to make their act a reality.

On the drive to Forever's place, they drank Cîroc right from the bottle. By the time she parked in front of her house, they were feeling the effects of the pilfered flavored alcohol and kush. Smoking and drinking always made Summer horny and silly. She spilled the drink on her blouse trying to mimic a few of Forever's dance moves.

"Oops. I made a mess and I got it on my shirt," Summer said, drunkenly stripping out of her top. "I don't got nothing to change into. I left my bag at work," she explained, now topless. Being around each other practically nude almost every day at work made it nothing to be like this in front of Forever.

"I see, and I guess you want mama to come clean you up?" Forever flirted, eyeing Summer's nude-topped body.

"Ummm. You made that sound good." Summer peeled off her cutoff jeans giving her a clear view of her clean shaved mound.

"Come here and show me how you can help," she said, sitting down on the cool leather chaise.

Forever had a lustful smirk on her face as she stripped out of her clothes. By the time she had disrobed, Summer was lying back on the soft, white leather loveseat with her fingers working her steaming pink pot. She skillfully rotated her slim hips in the same motion inviting Forever to join in at any time. Forever trampled over to the chaise and straddled Summer's thigh as she fell on top of her. They kissed, sucked, bumped, and grinded until their uncontrollable waves of passion overtook them.

Summer rolled them off of the chaise onto the soft carpeted floor. A half hour later, wasted and lost in sexual bliss, they fell asleep while wrapped in each other's arms. And a short time after that, the sound of Summer's cell phone pulled Forever out of her sleep. She tried to wake Summer, but she wouldn't. So Forever answered her phone.

"Hello? Hey, what's up, Free?"

"Where's Summer?"

"She's asleep and won't get up. I tried when I saw it was you calling."

"She's asleep. Who is this?"

"This is Forever. We at my house," Forever answered, rushing into the bathroom to pee.

"What's she doing asleep at your crib?"

"We got pretty wasted at the club tonight. She asked me to drop her off at home, but as you can see, we didn't make it," she giggled.

"Tell that bitch it's me on the phone, and give it to her ass now!" he snapped, getting loud on the phone.

"Hold on." She walked over to her friend when she came out of the bathroom "Summer! Summer!" she called out her name while patting her on the leg.

"Nooo, just a few more minutes. Leave me alone; I'm tired."

"Girl, Free's on the phone. You better wake up and get on this fuckin' phone before he comes over here and taps that ass!"

The mention of Freebandz coming there made her get up and get on the phone.

"Hello, bae, don't be mad at me. I was calling and texting you to come get me from work, but you didn't answer," Summer explained, sounding guilty. Forever prayed that she didn't tell him that they came to her house and got drunk after she just lied to him about getting drunk at the club.

"I know, but I got sick all over my clothes in the car, so Forever brought me here so she could wash 'em for me and we could sober up. I guess I just passed out," she lied.

"Bitch, how many times I told your dumb ass about drinking like that?"

"I know, bae, stop. Don't be mad, please. I got

the rest of the money we needed," she pleaded, rolling her eyes and hoping the mention of the money would calm him down.

"What would you have done if she wasn't at work tonight or if you had some more money lined up? Bitch, answer me that."

"Free, you know how they've been robbing them cabs lately, so I was scared to get in one," Summer said, not knowing that her man was part of the crew behind the latest string of cab robberies. "I'm sorry, bae, don't be mad."

Forever had eased out of the room and returned without Summer knowing. She had a long thick vibrator in her hand that she went and got from her bedside drawer. Forever ran the tip of it up Summer's inner thigh slowly before clicking it to life.

"Ummm!" Summer moaned, then tried to squirm away and mouthed for Forever to stop it because she was still on the phone.

Forever ignored her and touched Summer's mound, causing her to twitch as she slid the toy over her clit. Summer let out another soft moan that Freebandz missed because he was too busy scolding her. She was so happy when he ordered her to get home and then hung up on her.

"Bout time he hung up," Forever said, smiling then licking the tip of the toy.

"Bitch, why you playing? I know you gotta get going, so stop wasting time and lay down," she said, waving the toy.

"You just don't know how he's been since that Mexican killed his guy and got away. I know he finna go in on me when I get there just from the way he sounded just now."

"I'ma give you three hundred for him; now shut the fuck up and enjoy yourself." Forever shushed her by sliding the toy all the way inside of her while working it slowly in and out of her as she sucked her tiny, hard, pearl-shaped nipples.

After Forever and Summer had drained themselves, Forever allowed Summer to take a quick shower and then dropped her off at home. On the drive, Forever asked a few more questions about the Mexican man and found out it was Jesse. As soon she pulled away from the projects, she called Byrd and asked him to meet her at her place as soon as he could. He was at her house before she even got home.

"What up? This better be 'bout something. You know this is around the time a nigga just be getting to sleep," Byrd said, looking at his icy gold Movado watch that read that it was 4:40 a.m.

"Just come in. I don't want nobody to see us talking out here," Forever told him as she walked past him and unlocked the door to her place. "Look behind you, please," she exclaimed while taking off her jacket.

"Ummm, I see the twins miss me," he joked, noticing her perky nipples poking out from under the satin shirt she was wearing.

"Byrd, let's be serious," she said, pulling off the

yoga pants she had put on to take Summer home.

"What you call me over for? Right now I'm looking at the best reason why," he said, staring at her butt that wasn't covered by the short shirt. The sight got him instantly aroused.

"Okay, but I'm not the reason I called you over here. I got some info on who tried to rob Jasso, and I'ma need some cash before I tell you," she told him, standing with her hand out and the other resting on her wide hip.

"It's worth five Gs if it's real."

"It is."

"How do I know that?"

"Cuz you know I don't play when it comes to money. Just give me some now and the rest when you check it out."

Byrd agreed, giving her the two thousand dollars that he had on him and promising her the rest afterward. She told him how she got the information from Summer that Freebandz was behind the murder and attempted robbery.

"And this bitch, Summer, she works with you on what days?"

"Almost every day. I can call you when she's there if you want me to. I know Freebandz drops her off and picks her up from work most of the time. So you can catch his ass in the parking lot."

"Yeah, you do that. Now, what's up with a shot of that pussy though?" he asked, gripping his hard-on through his jeans.

"I ain't fuckin', but I can give you some head," she offered.

Byrd agreed, pulling out his length for her to wrap her warm lips around. While she went to work sucking him off, he texted the info she gave him to Asad. Asad told him to come pick up the reward money that was being offered later, and Byrd told him that all he wanted was the cash back that he paid Forever because, like him, all he wanted was justice for Casey.

CHAPTER 5

It was a little after eight in the morning when Zay made it safely back to Milwaukee. He had just spent the night sitting up in a lonely truck stop waiting for Miguel with Jasso's monthly shipment from Luis. Then he drove through the night, slapping himself a few times to stay awake and watching every set of headlights that got too close behind him.

Zay was now back home but beaten down by exhaustion from his journey through the state of Illinois. He could hardly stand up in the shower as he scrubbed away the smell of diesel and stale Black & Mild smoke that clung to him. The young thug thought of what Jasso told him, and he knew he needed to be at 100 percent in order to carry out the boss's orders when he woke up. Zay believed the punishment for murdering an innocent was death. It was the only true compensation for robbing one of his loved ones, and he planned on collecting the lives owed for taking Casey from Jasso and her family.

Everyone should know by now that the streets do talk, and they told Zay that he could find the ones he was hunting at Silks almost any night of the week. But it wasn't until the second night that Zay stalked out of the popular strip club, that he caught sight of Freebandz in the car that Jasso had given him a description of.

Zay checked his watch. It was nine forty-five in the afternoon, yet it was still early enough for the parking lot to be open, so he could sit and watch

Freebandz and Summer fool around in the Impala. What he didn't know was that she was a player in a lot of Freebandz's robberies. Zay eased out of the backseat of his gray Chevy Trailblazer that he had stolen earlier that day and made his way over to his target.

The two were so caught up in their quickie that neither of them noticed the messenger of death standing right outside the window. Just as Freebandz was about to release his load down Summer's throat, Zay snatched the door open and savagely rained down on his victim's face, breaking his nose along with a few teeth. Zay then clamped an arm around Freebandz's neck and attempted to pull him out of the seat. Freebandz fought to keep his consciousness as he struggled with his attacker. He tried desperately to reach his gun under the driver's seat as the hold continued to tighten around his neck. Zay wanted to choke him unconscious so he could take him somewhere and kill him slowly.

"Let him go!" Summer snapped out of her shock and snatched the gun up under the seat and took shaky aim at Zay.

"Fuck you, bitch!" Zay said as he pulled Freebandz out of the car.

Summer saw this and started shooting wildly at him. Zay quickly dropped behind the back door. He pulled out his second gun and sent shots into the body of Freebandz while firing a few at Summer before he made his getaway. Zay heard the stripper let out a scream that told him his job was well done. Once he was safely back inside the Trailblazer, he promised not to play with the next one, so he drove away from the scene to swoop back into his own car that he parked not far from the club.

After wiping the SUV down, out of caution, he left it running just in case he needed to run back to it. Then he jogged over to his car and drove it back to the club to watch the action while he waited on Forever to come out of the sleazy establishment. He found a parking spot that both gave him a clear view of the scene surrounding the Impala and was far enough that he would go unnoticed. Zay backed the dark tan-and-gold Dodge Charger that he had rolling on twenty-three-inch forged rims into the slot just in case he had to pull out in a hurry. Then he texted Forever on his burner phone telling her that he was there outside and that he didn't want to stay because of all of the police activity that was going on outside of the club.

A short time later, and Forever, along with most

of the crowd in Silks, flooded out into the parking lot to be nosey. Zay pulled alongside of Forever and tapped his horn once to get her attention. Many of the others in the crowd looked his way as well, but he wasn't worried because he wasn't the only one trying to get away from the barricade of flashing lights of police and EMS vehicles that filled that end of the parking lot.

"You riding with me, or you staying here to answer questions?"

Zay already knew she was coming with him because she wanted the rest of the money that Asad had promised her for the information she had given them.

"No, boo! I don't talk to no police. They might have some shit on my ass for all I know."

"I want to put something on that ass, if you

going?" he said, eyeing her big legs that sparkled from the shimmering body lotion she had on for her stage show that was cut short because of the murder.

"If you can do something with lil' daddy, then, yeah. But if you can't handle it, you can just take a bitch to the crib," Forever flirted with him, but she had no idea she was face-to-face with death in the flesh.

"I can show you better!" he told her as she got out of the car and then went back into the club to get her things. "Why not smash that sexy ass before I kill it? When you're dead you can't run your mouth to nobody," he said out loud to no one. He then looked out the window and saw the police trying to make sense of what the murder was about.

When Forever got back into the car, Zay pulled off and headed to the nearest and cheapest motel he could find.

"Aye, you can just give me that cash you're about to spend on a room and head to my place," Forever suggested, because she thought the bad feeling she had in her just was that he would make her find her way home from the motel after he was through with her.

"Sounds like a plan to me, as long as you ain't got no nigga there waiting on you," he said, already knowing that she lived alone from the information Asad and Byrd gave him about her.

"Never that. I like repeat customers, and I can't afford for you to put me out there as some punk bitch. That's bad for business," she said, rubbing the print in his jeans from his hard-on.

Once Zay and Forever got behind the closed doors of her apartment, they tore at each other, letting items of clothing fall wherever they landed. Zay had popped half a Viagra just before he pulled up to the 38th Street apartment building, without her knowing. He had plans on giving her the best fuck of her life before he ended it. After a two-hour sexathon, Zay caught her off guard with a right cross to the jaw that knocked her out. Then he placed her in the bathtub, filled it with water, and cut deeply into both of her wrists before holding her head underwater until she stopped fighting. He wanted it to look like a suicide when someone found her.

Zay took his time cleaning up the place and writing a note on her cell phone that read, "I'm so sorry, I can't do this anymore . . . Bye." When he was satisfied with his work, he casually left the apartment and went home.

CHAPTER 6

Reruns of the television show House played on the fifty-five-inch screen in Fame's bedroom, but he wasn't watching the show. His mind was on other things that were going wrong in his life. He thought back to the day when Drew showed up at Promiss's house. She did look surprised to see him standing on her porch, but then Fame saw her leaving work with Drew later that day. Fame's jealousy made him confront himself with questions that made him sit at home alone on a hype Friday night. He didn't want Promiss to know that she had this effect on him, that she made him question his place in her life. Promiss's set ringtone sounded, snapping Fame out of his thoughts. He didn't move to pick up the phone; he let it go to voicemail for the third day in a row. He didn't want to hear whatever story she had to tell him about the man she had been spending time with. No, he just turned his back on it and went to sleep wondering if things were or weren't as they seemed to be with her.

~ ~ ~

Danny Boy woke up slightly hungover from buying the bar the night before. He couldn't place where he was as he looked around the dimly illuminated motel room, then at the woman asleep beside him in the full-size bed. She had one arm over her face, but he knew from her light skin that she wasn't Forever or his baby mama, Matisha. So without waking her, Danny Boy eased out of the bed, went into the bathroom, relieved himself, and then splashed cold water on his face to try to clear the fog from his hangover. When he looked at his watch, he remembered that it was his little brother's birthday. Pain stabbed his heart, and he thought back on his days when he was younger and him and Jon would wake up extra early then race into the kitchen to see who could eat the most Frosted Flakes before they went outside to play.

Jon didn't have a care in the world as long as he was with his big brother. Now their mom and dad were throwing a block party in his memory on his birthday. Danny Boy still didn't know who killed Jon, nor why, and the guilt was eating him up inside. He took a quick hoe bath, dressed, and left a few bills on the table beside the door for Ms. Sleeping Beauty to catch a cab home, before he walked out the door. Danny Boy looked around the lot and couldn't find his car. That's when he remembered he rode there with her. He cursed himself for being drunk and for his cell phone being dead.

~ ~ ~

Slim sat in his car rolling up his first blunt of the day in the motel parking lot. The sun was up, and he had a feeling that it was going to be a hot day from how warm the morning was. Slim started the car then turned the air conditioner on low. In his peripheral vision he saw a guy walking his way. Slim eased his gun from its stash place under the dashboard and placed it under his leg before lowering the window to see what the guy wanted with him.

"Aye, fam, you wanna sell some of that load?" Danny Boy asked, stopping a few feet from the car.

"Man, bro, this it right here, bro, and I ain't tryna come off it. My day just wouldn't be right if I did."

"Yeah, I know what you mean. Mine already startin' off fucked up. I'm stuck at this bitch cuz I rode with a broad I met at the club and some drunk shit last night. My battery's dead on my phone, so I can't call nobody for a ride, and to top it all off I don't got shit to smoke on," Danny Boy vented.

"I'll tell ya what. Give ten bucks and I'll drop you off?" Slim offered.

"But, shit, here's a dub." Danny Boy peeled the twenty-dollar bill off of the small bankroll and handed it to him then got in the car. "You just saved my life, and you got the same phone I do. Do you mind if I get a quick charge?"

"Nawl, go ahead."

"Shit, fam, you my new ace in the hole."

"Where your car at?" Slim asked, keeping his hand close to the gun just in case his good deed turned bad.

"It should be parked outside Passion's. I got my keys, so it should be there. I got fuckin' wasted last night, or that bitch slipped me something, cuz I don't remember shit really."

"It's cool. I'm going down that way. Do you see spots or anything like that? If you do, then, yeah, she got you, but if not you was just wasted."

"Nawl, I don't see spots. This feels like a regular ole hangover. Good looking for this though."

"It ain't no biggie. It's only a few blocks over from where I'm heading anyway." Slim lit the blunt before turning into traffic in Silver Spring's eastbound lanes. He didn't feel Danny Boy was on bullshit. "Aye, fam, what they call you?" he asked between puffs.

"Jack Daniels or JD, whichever is easier to remember," he answered, because he didn't really know how he was going to fool with Slim just yet.

"Jack Daniels? Man, that's why your ass needs a ride now!" Slim joked, and then they laughed.

The two thugs hit it off right away. It was like they were meant to meet one another. They polished off the blunt while listening to the gangster trap music sounds of Baby Drew and Coo Coo Cal, Milwaukee's own cocaine cowboys. When they turned onto the block where Danny Boy's car was parked, it was right where he had left it along with a nice good-morning parking ticket on the windshield.

"Now that's just wrong right there. They say they don't want you to drive drunk, but when you don't, they give you a phat-ass ticket anyway," Slim said, pulling up beside his car.

"Yeah, it gotta be someone a nigga can talk to about that shit, fam." Danny Boy laughed with him. "Thanks again, fam. We having a block party on 19th and Hopkins later. You should swing by and fuck with ya boy," he said, pressing the disarm button on his remote. Then he waited as the car beeped and started up for him.

"Fo show. I'll swing through. I wanna try some

of that loud you say you got anyways. I'm always looking for something new. I'ma weed connoisseur." Slim grinned as they pounded fists and exchanged phone numbers.

"Slim? Hold up!" Danny Boy shouted, stopping Slim from pulling off. He remembered that he had two sacks of weed in his car.

"Here, I got something for ya right now. Tell me how you like this here." He tossed Slime one of the sacks of kush through the window then got in his car.

"Will do." Slim held it to his nose. "It smell like it's that fire! In a minute, bro bro!" he said. Then they parted ways.

CHAPTER 7

Promiss was curious and desperate to know why Fame wasn't answering or returning her calls and texts. She guessed it had to have something to do with Drew showing up out of the blue the way he had. And if that's the case then Fame needed to allow her to explain things. She left her sister and Shay to break down and package up the six hundred pounds of kush weed that was delivered to them in the middle of the night, to go have a talk with her man. If Fame was still that, Promiss thought as she drove to his house. Promiss tried his number again once she had parked in front of his house.

Both of his cars were in the driveway, one behind the other so he could pull his old-school out of the garage. She got out of her car and walked up to the door and rang the doorbell two quick times. While she waited a car pulled into the driveway and a tall shapely older woman got out and walked toward her.

"Good morning! Who are you looking for?" the woman asked when she was standing in front of Promiss.

"Hi. I'm looking for Fame. Who are you?" Promiss asked, trying to think of who the woman reminded her of, but jealousy would not let her think clearly at the moment.

"Who am I?" She smiled.

"I'm sorry, I didn't know."

The mother waved the apology off and unlocked the door and called out to Fame as they walked inside the house. She wasn't worried about him having another woman over because Fame didn't bring women home that he wasn't serious about.

"Ma, that's you? I'm in the shower. I'll be out in a minute," Fame exclaimed from the bathroom.

"Okay. I got Promiss out here with me, boy, so hurry up!" she said, heading toward the kitchen.

"Who?"

"Promiss, boy, you heard me."

"I meant what is she doing here?" He paused. "I'll be right out." Fame finished up his shower, threw on some basketball shorts and a black wifebeater, and then went to find that his mother and Promiss were at the sink washing dishes. "Good morning!" he greeted as he walked up and gave his mother a kiss on the cheek.

"Boy, how many time do I gotta tell you to wash

out your dishes when you're done with them? Please tell me why you have a dishwasher if you're not going to use it."

"I do use it, Ma. I just been busy, and I forgot to do 'em last night."

"Unless you had company over here, she is washing more than just last night's. And why haven't you been answering that girl's calls? You got her over here worried about you." His mother cut right into him as she made breakfast for him.

"I just needed some alone time, Ma. She had something that she needed to work out," he answered, looking Promiss directly in her eyes as he did.

"I understand. That's kinda why I'm here this morning. I needed to be around you for a bit and get out of that house. I'm trying to deal with shit and make it through the days without crying. I've been shedding tears ever since Dr. Nissin told us about your father's condition," the mother explained, getting emotional.

~ ~ ~

Slim pulled up to Fame's house, and as he approached the door, he noticed that it was slightly ajar. He drew his gun, paused to listen, then crept on inside knowing it was unlike his friend to be slipping like this.

"Fame? Where you at?" he called out, making his way through the house. Slim spotted Promiss before she saw him, and put his gun away. Then he almost ran face-to-face with Fame.

"Damn it! What up?"

"Y'all need to learn how to lock the door. Y'all actin' like this ain't the ghetto," Slim scolded them before he noticed Fam's mother standing over the stove.

"Boy, you better speak to me before you come in here talking that mess," she checked him.

"Awwwe . . . You know I would never not speak to you, ma'am. I didn't see you. Good morning!"

"What up, everybody! What are we eating?" Byrd asked as he walked up behind Slim then went and hugged Fame's mother.

"Bro, wasn't you just saying some shit to me about not having the door behind him was because if something was wrong, he could get out fast."

"You better watch your mouth around me, boy!"

"I'm sorry, Ma!"

Slim swiped a strip of turkey bacon from the dish next to the stove. Once the big breakfast was done, the mother gave her son a hug and kiss on the cheek.

"Promiss, come walk me to my car." The wise mother had noticed how her son was acting toward Promiss and wanted to have a word with her alone. "That boy loves you. Do you know that?"

"Yes ma'am. I know, and I love him just as much as he do me if not more. It's been too long since I've had a real man in my life."

"I hear you. That's why when you get a hold of that one that's meant for you, you do what you must to hold on to him and hold on for dear life." She stopped beside her car door. "I can see that it's something going on with you two. I can see hurt in his eyes. Woman to woman, Promiss, I can also see confusion in yours."

"Ma'am I . . . "

"Hold up. This I'm saying is for you to hear, not speak," she said, cutting Promiss off. "I've been where you are now. I was torn between two men. But I went with my heart, not what I was used to. And I'm so glad I did. Sure we had some hard times, but after all off the partying and whores, I still got him, and I don't regret my choice."

"I hear you. I'm not going nowhere. Fame hasn't given me a reason to regret nothing yet. It's just someone from my past suddenly popped up, and I haven't had a chance to sit down and talk to Fame about him really. I know should've sooner, but I really didn't expect to see him again."

"Promiss, I'm not the one you need to say this to. Don't let that boy get away from you today without y'all talking. I know my son, and he don't like putting his emotions out there, so you gotta do it for him." They hugged, and Promiss watched her get in the car and pull off before going back into the house.

When she returned to the kitchen, she overheard Slim saying he was invited to a block party later. Promiss turned her attention to Fame, who was already on his second helping of food.

"Excuse me, y'all. Boo, before you go out and play with your friends, we need to talk."

"Well, that's my cue," Byrd said, making a sandwich with the last of his omelet.

"Y'all go head and talk. We'll just see you at the block party," Slim said, forking the last of his second helping into his mouth then getting up from the table and following Byrd out of the house.

Once alone, Promiss went into her story surrounding her and Drew's relationship. Fame said nothing, nor did he stop eating while she talked.

"So where does all that leave us, Promiss?" he asked when she sat quietly.

"I want to be where my heart is, and that's with you. I just need time to close things up with him. I feel like I owe him that much."

"You don't owe him shit. He left you, and not the other way around."

"Boo."

"I'm just sayin'. But you go ahead and do what you gotta do. I'm not going to play a fucking waiting game for too long. Know that, Promiss," he said as he cleared the table and gave her a joyless kiss on her forehead before walking away from her and into his bedroom to get dressed.

Promiss rinsed and put the few dishes into the dishwasher. Then she went into the bedroom behind him. He was standing nude when she entered the room, so she walked up and squeezed his butt before wrapping her arms around his waist.

"Girl, you better stop," he warned, unable to stay mad at her when she had her body pressed tightly against his.

"I got your 'girl.' You're my shit. I do what I want when I wanna," she told him, then started planting gentle kisses up and down his back while slowly stroking his length with her small warm hands.

Promiss turned him to face her, and as soon as she had him nice and hard, she kissed his lips, dropped to her knees, and took him into her mouth. She wondered if he had stood there nude because he knew she could not resist him that way. As she sucked, he peeled her out of her shirt and bra. Fame wanted to feel her cumming on him while looking into her pretty brown eyes. So he scooped her up and tossed her onto the bed. Then he helped her out of her jeans and panties and pushed his hardness deep inside of her warmth. Promiss gasped, and he covered her mouth with his hand as he slowly, pacingly sawed in and out of her. Promiss held on to him digging her nails into his back, and he hurt her so good.

"I love you. Yes! Fame, I love you!" she sang.

CHAPTER 8

The day was bright, perfect, not too hot or cool.

Nineteenth Street was blocked off on both ends by white-and-orange wooden roadblock stands and packed with people, family and friends. Both young and older kids ran through the sheltered street to the games set up. Many of Jon's loved ones wore RIP airbrushed shirts with his picture on them. Mr. Mays brought out two ice cream trucks and parked one on each end of the block party, making them free to the children. Other relatives and coworkers manned the grills and served food and drinks. Milwaukee's DJ

Homer Blow played the hits.

Danny Boy's parents worked the party, greeting people who gave them cards and flowers of sympathy. All in all, people were having a good time laughing at funny memories of Jon and telling personal stories of him in remembrance of the fallen son. Danny Boy sat with his baby's mama on his lap and a cold draft beer in his hand watching the movements of the party-goers. He and his people were ready for whatever. All knowing how quickly things can turn from the sound of laughter and hands clapping, to that of screams and gunfire. Danny Boy's baby mama had a bad feeling, and if her instincts were right, something bad was going to go down. He prayed she was wrong and that she was only trying to keep him by her side away from the females that were trying their best to get his attention.

~ ~ ~

Byrd, Zay, Slim, Asad, and a few others all circled the blocks swinging and showing off their colorful custom vehicles before parking and joining the party. To their surprise the block party was for the young thug they had killed. Byrd was the one to call Fame, who had just texted him and said he was parked at the opposite end of the block.

"Bro, this shit here is for that lil nigga. Look at the shirts."

"Who you talking about?" Fame asked, looking around for someone that could give him a view of their T-shirt.

"The one from the basement party, feel me?"

"What!" he said just as he got a clear look at the face on a group of girls' shirts jumping rope not far from him. "Where y'all at?"

"We over here by the school. Where you?" Byrd asked as he put his gun on his waist under his shirt.

"I'ma make my way to y'all, just hold tight. I'm walking," he said and ended the call as he weaved his way through the crowded maze of people, on alert for his enemy.

~ ~ ~

Danny Boy recognized Slim standing in a group of guys that weren't from his hood, but he knew from their fancy whips that he had seen floating around the city. He made his way over to Slim. Fame looked up and recognized Danny Boy as the shooter that he had fought with at the lakefront on his first date with Promiss. Fame took off in a sprint down the block to catch up to Danny Boy. Something in Danny Boy's gut told him to look over his shoulder, but by the time the face of the man running toward him registered, it was too late. Fame's hard fist had caught Danny Boy in the back of his head, and a quick right cross to the jaw staggered him. But Danny Boy didn't fall. He reached for his weapon on his waist that wasn't there. He had put the gun in the house earlier when the police rode through on their bikes just to let everyone know that they were watching them.

Just as Danny Boy got his feet back under him, one of his guys ran to his aid. Eshy caught Fame the same way that Fame had done to Danny Boy. That's when the others joined in. Byrd was the first to see them fighting and took off in an all-out sprint to help Fame with the other right behind him. Zay was the one who saw one of Danny Boy's guy's grab a chopper from under the porch of an abandoned house and let it ride. Sending shots at Byrd and his guys, people screamed and ran for cover. The three bike cops took aim at Zay and the others, yelling for them to stand down.

That's when Slim and one of Danny Boy's guys started shooting at the police. They dropped one of the officers before he could take cover behind the ice cream truck with his buddies. Danny Boy's dad, Mr. Mays, saw his son was in trouble and pulled his .357

Magnum out and then let off two shots in the air to get the attention of the two guys jumping his son. Mr. Mays didn't want to risk hitting his son, so as soon as one of the guys turned his way, he shot him. The father was not trying to bury another son. Soon the MPD's swat team swarmed in from almost all directions.

Fame knew he couldn't make it back to his car, so he just turned and ran up Akinison, trying to get away from the two goons and the police that were hot on his heels.

~ ~ ~

Drew was just pulling away from Kentucky Fried Chicken's drive-thru window with his hot order of spicy chicken and wedges when he saw two guys with guns chasing another man up the street. As they got closer, he saw that the man being chased was Promiss's boyfriend. Drew tossed his food bag onto the backseat and made a wide, hard, U-turn and raced after Fame to pick him up.

When Fame was cut off by the car, he thought he was a goner. His clip was empty, but he still had a tight grip on his gun from the adrenaline that was rushing through his body.

"Get in! Come on, get the fuck in!" Drew shouted from his window.

Fame was shocked to see who had come to his rescue, but not stupid enough to turn him down either. He practically dived into the passenger seat as Drew sped off in the direction that he saw Fame running from.

"Fuck. Good lookin', man," Fame thanked him as he tried to catch his breath.

"What they at you for, fam?"

"Some bullshit that jumped off at a block party," he answered, not seeing the need in putting Drew in his business even though he just saved his life. "Hey, bend this right here. I got my car parked down that street."

Drew did as he was told and took Fame to his car. They didn't see anyone that looked like they needed to be concerned with by the car, so Fame got out.

"You good?"

"Yeah, I'm good from here. Good lookin', man. I owe you one. I'll have Promiss get up with you for me so I can hit your hand for this." Fame got

out and ran to his car before Drew could protest.

Drew made another U-turn because there were

too many police cars ahead in the other direction and

he couldn't afford to get pulled over with the gun and

half ounce of kush that he had on him. Just as he

reached the middle of the block, out of nowhere,

three gunmen sprayed his car with hot lead. Drew

was hit several times and lost control of his car. He

crashed into the side of the corner store. The shooters

ran up on the wreck and made sure he didn't live

through it.

All Fame could do was watch as the man that just

saved his life lost his own in a street war that he knew

nothing about.

"Damn! Damn! Damn!" He made a promise to make somebody pay for Drew's death, then raced away from the scene. Fame pulled his phone out and called back the first missed caller on his screen. Byrd answered, demanding that Fame tell him where he was because the last time he had seen Fame was when he was being chased down the street. Fame told him that he was okay and in his car. They agreed to all meet up on Eleventh and Concordia before going to swap out of their cars just to see how everyone made it out before they made anymore moves.

CHAPTER 9

After the block party remains had been cleaned up and the police and the rest of the first responders had cleared off the block, Mr. Mays along with a couple of his most trusted friends, all sat in the garage drinking beer and talking about the deadly pandemonium that ruined Jon's memorial with Danny Boy.

"Pop, I promise you I don't know what this shit's about. I don't even know that punk that snaked me."

"Danny, you had to have, because he came straight at you. So you better think and get to talking," a friend of his father said.

"Unc, I met that light-skin dude this morning. It wasn't nothing. He gave me a ride to my car, and I told him to drop by here for the party. That's it. I didn't know he was even with the nigga I was boxing with until everybody jumped in," he explained as honestly as he could while holding an icepack on his swollen face.

Danny Boy's stepdad wasn't so old that he didn't have an ear in the streets. Mr. Mays knew well how Danny Boy and his friends got down out there.

"Danny, let me tell you what I know, and then maybe we can walk down that bullshit that happened today from there," Mr. Mays exclaimed from on top of the deep freezer where he sat while nursing a beer.

"Tell me what you know 'bout what! I'm telling you this ain't on me, Pop."

"So you wasn't paid by some white bitch to take

out her husband?"

"How did you . . . ?"

"Shut up and let me finish! I know you did the deed for her, but some other shit went down that day too. Now tell me what that shit was about," he said, looking his stepson dead in his eyes.

"Who told you about my business?"

"Don't ask me shit, boy! Just answer the muthafuckin' question!"

Danny Boy wondered if his brother had spilled the beans about the hit he took him on. Jon wasn't supposed to be a part of it; they were just together when the best opportunity to get the husband opened. But if Jon would've told him about it, why wouldn't he have said anything sooner? So Danny Boy quickly thought to play it safe.

"Well, since you know all that. I followed the

dude for two or three days trying to catch the best time to get him. Then one day he didn't go to his job or whatever. His ass went fishing down at the docks with another white dude that I'd saw him with a few times. I think they work together. Anyways, I did what I was paid to do, but he must've had this nigga on his team or . . ."

"Or that nigga thought you was at his head, so he got at you," his uncle finished for him. "I was across the street when I saw that it was you being chased that day."

"Aww, damn," Danny Boy said, surprised. "So, Pop, what now?"

"Why you asking me? You made this mess, lil nigga. Now we get it right!"

"So y'all think the same nigga that caused all that shit today was the one that killed Jon?"

"There ain't no question about if it was him today. But I don't know if he had anything to do with your brother. That's still in the air."

"Why you say that?"

"Because he would've just come at you a long time ago. I don't believe these the same ones behind that. He didn't know your brother; he knows you."

"Didn't you said that you know one of 'em?" the uncle asked.

"Yeah, I met him today at the motel."

"Well, call him and see if we can get a sit-down with him and his guys to try and put an end to this," Mr. Mays suggested.

"Alright. When you want me to call him?"

"Shit, call his ass now before somebody else gets killed."

Danny Boy picked up his phone and did as he

was told. He really didn't think Slim would answer his cell because of all that had gone down. He was just about to end the call because of how long it had rung and send a text asking if they could talk, when Slim answered his phone.

~ ~ ~

The beautiful sunny day slowly transformed into a monstrous stormy evening. Promiss didn't mind the rainy nights. The wet murkiness only bothered her when it was accompanied by high winds, thunder clapping, and blinding lighting. She hated to be alone on those nights. Ever since she could remember, she had been afraid of storms.

Promiss was tucked securely in bed with the volume of the television show that she was trying to use to keep her mind off the chaos outside on high. When she heard the sound of her doorbell, she wasn't expecting company in this weather but she was happy to find that it was Fame standing on her porch.

"Hey, boo, you must've heard my prayers," she said, allowing him inside. When he didn't respond, the look on his face concerned her. "What's going on with you? What's wrong?" Promiss asked as he took off his soaked hoody.

"I gotta tell you something messed up, and I'd rather you hear it from me first."

"Oookay . . . What is it?"

"Ahhgh!" he exclaimed, not allowing her to take them from his hand. "I don't know how to say this shit."

"Fame, just tell me what you got to say, cuz you're scaring me."

She stepped away from him.

"Let's sit down," Fame said, seeing the fear on

her face.

"Just tell me. I don't wanna sit down!" she snapped.

"Promiss, Drew got killed today."

"Drew? What Drew? Who you talking about, Fame?" she asked, already moving toward her phone.

"Your friend Drew." He walked over to her and stopped her from dialing. "Who you calling? Put the phone down. I wouldn't play with you about nothing like this."

"Fame, how do you know?" she asked with a tone to her voice and shaking uncontrollably.

"Don't. Don't think it. He saved my life and got killed as he drove away. It all should be on the news right now. Th-there wasn't anything I could do to help him. The police was right there. I had to get away."

Promiss was in shock. She couldn't find her words, and after a few short moments the first of her tears rolled down her cheeks. Even though she didn't want to get back together with Drew, she still cared for him, and the news of his death hurt. She allowed Fame to pull her into his arms and hold her. Promiss buried her face in his chest soaking Fame's shirt with the tears she had for her past lover.

"What do you mean he saved your life? What was y'all doing together?" she asked, looking him in the eyes.

Fame didn't want to give her the bad news. He didn't know how to tell her what she wanted to know. So he took a deep breath and explained how everything went down, step by step. He didn't hold anything back knowing that she needed to know in order to find closure enough to move on. The only thing Fame was unable to answer for her was why the guy was shooting at him at the docks in the first place.

~ ~ ~

Slim was just walking out of the bathroom when he heard his phone ringing and vibrating on the pool table where it was charging.

"Aye, y'all, this that nigga JD calling me now!" he exclaimed when he saw the name on the screen of his phone.

"Who?" Byrd asked, watching Slim press Answer on his phone.

"The one Fame got at today at the block party."

"Put him on speaker."

"What up?" Slim answered as the room hushed to hear what was about to be said.

"Say, Slim, man. I don't know what all his beef your mans got with me, but I'm calling to try to put an end to it before more of us get tagged. Feel me?" said Danny Boy.

"Yeah, I feel ya on that. But from what I hear you the one that got something with bro. You busted first down at the lake, remember that?"

"Man, that's why I'm trying to holla at him in person and without bullshit. Can you ask him to meet up with me?"

"He ain't around me right now, but, yeah, I can do that. When and where do you wanna do this?"

Slim and the others listened as Danny Boy asked his old man when and where would be a good place for them to meet up with them on 36th and Fon Du Lac in the open parking lot across from the area's frantic police station. That way things between them would stay on the up-and-up. As he and Danny Boy ironed out the details, Byrd was texting Fame what was going on, so when Fame texted back agreeing to the meet, he told him to set it up for some time in the next few days because he was dealing with Promiss and was not in a rush to talk with them. Byrd held his phone up for Slim to see the response and take it from there.

"Alright, so around noon the day after tomorrow. I'll see y'all then."

"Fo sho," Slim confirmed, then ended the call before anything more could be said. He didn't want Danny Boy to think he would try to side with him when the time came.

"I hope them fools don't think its safe for them cuz the police gon' be right across the street," Sharky said while rolling a blunt.

"I hope not cuz that nigga Asad got a spot right around the corner on the same block as that punk-ass station," Byrd said, texting Fame back. "So I hope they know we will get it crackin' on top of that muthafuckin' station."

"I think he know that we get down whenever and wherever. If not he gon' learn the deadly way if they come on some bullshit," Slim said, accepting the blunt from Byrd's young goon and sparking it up.

"So, Big Byrd, is we still going over to Zarkos for ladies' night?"

"Shit! Thanks for reminding me, Sharky. I gotta let Zay know we ain't going to make it. Too much shit going on to be out in the streets right now."

Slim agreed that they should chill and stay in just in case some more mess jumped off. The police were out looking for them any, questioning people from the block party and witnesses that went down and gave the police helpful information on them. The storm had let up, so he was going to hook up with Shay for the rest of the night, if he could.

CHAPTER 10

Early morning social media friends and followers were in a hot gossiping frenzy when the news hit of Zay's body being found in an apartment building on Wells Street. The scene on all of the Milwaukee news shows showed the outside of the apartment building that was almost surrounded by the MPD, news crews, and a bunch of nosey people that were being kept back by lines of yellow crime scene tape. The gruesome double homicide was discovered by two teenagers in one of the vacant units.

Slim had chosen the perfect person when he chose Shay to lay low for a couple of days with, because all of her social media friends knew she would love to hear all the gossip surrounding the violent burden of someone as popular as Zay. So they made sure Shay did, and as soon as she did, she informed Slim. When she had finished telling him and letting him read the posts on her page and few of her inbox messages, he shut down on her for a while.

Shay let him be, guessing from the way he had taken the news that he must have been close to Zay or the other man that was found in the building that no one said anything about. After awhile he got up, still naked from the night before, and went into the bathroom. As soon as he did, his phone rang, and he told her to answer it through the closed door.

"Hello? Where y'all at, fam. We're here," Danny Boy said as soon as Slim's line was answered. Instead of taking it as disrespect when nobody showed up for the meeting, he decided to call and see

what had happened.

"Excuse me, who are you looking for?" asked

Shay when she answered.

"Oh, damn! Is this Slim's phone?"

"Yeah. Who's calling?"

"Let me speak to him. Tell him it's the person he

was supposed to meet with today," Danny Boy told

her, not trusting the unknown female with his name.

"I'll tell him to call you back another time. He

just lost a good friend and don't want to be bothered

with anything right now," she explained since he so

rudely ignored her question.

"Oh, I didn't know," Danny Boy said, wondering

if Slim's sudden loss had anything to do with the

situation that Eshy and him handled the night before.

"Tell him to get up with me as soon as he can so we

can get our big misunderstanding cleared up and that I'm sorry for his loss."

"Will do. Bye!" she said, ending the call.

Shay replaced the phone on the bedside table, wondering what kind of big misunderstanding Slim had with the caller. Shay knew that since she and Slim were only friends with benefits that it would no longer be too beneficial for her if she started prying into his personal life. Especially if she ever wanted them to become more than friends.

"Who was it?" he asked, already having an idea because of the ringtone. He liked Shay, so he was testing her to see how she acted after he allowed her to answer his phone. If she was too nosey, he didn't plan on spending any more nights with her because in his line of work, nosey girlfriends were very dangerous.

"He didn't say. Just for you to get up with him as soon as you can and that he's sorry for your loss. I told him that you didn't wanna be bothered because you had just lost your friend."

"Why you tell him that?" he asked, sitting down beside her on the bed.

"Because he said you missed a meeting with him and cuz it's the truth. You need to grieve and let me take care of you for the rest of the day. Slim, things don't have to be only about sex with us," she told him with a sexy little grin.

"That's good to know, but right now it's what I need to help take my mind off everything. I don't wanna think of shit else but how good you feel and sound when I make you cum."

"Is that right?" she asked as she lay back on the cool black padded leather headboard of her plush queen-sized bed.

"Don't think then." She smiled, opening her legs to him.

Slim took the invite as a summons to put his tongue to use for something other than talking about what he wanted to do to her. He rolled over onto the bed and crawled between her knees, pushing them up with his shoulders until he was face-to-face with her smooth mound.

"Umm, you already wet," he whispered without taking his eyes off of his target. Slim used his fingers to part her slit and then ran his long tongue over and around her swollen clit. Shay's eyes rolled, and she bit down on her pouty bottom lip trying not to let him know he had her right where he told her that he wanted her. But with the way he was licking on her she couldn't hold back her nymphomania any longer.

"Fuck yesss!" she exclaimed, clawing her thighs and anything else she could get her hands on.

Slim pushed two fingers into her warmth, sawing them skillfully in and out of her as his tongue went round and round on her button. Soon he could feel her body's quake building and building as Shay got wetter and louder. His length was so hard it hurt, but he wasn't ready to give it to her just yet. When he felt her trying to clamp her legs shut to slow the intense pleasure he was giving her with his tongue, he stopped, dragged her underneath him, and shoved his hardness deep inside her wetness. Slim held it there as the spasms of her orgasm made her buck her hips wildly. When she slowed, he started to match Shay's thrusts with long hard ones of his own until he had taken back control of their fuck fest. He pounded and pounded until Shay locked her legs around his waist forcing him to feel her muscles clench and unclench his hardness until she felt him releasing as she let go for the second time with him deep inside her.

CHAPTER 11

"Hey, girl, what you up to?" Shay asked, making her way over to Slim.

"Hey yourself," Endure responded to her cousin. "I'ma 'bout to open a joint account for me and Sharky. Aren't you supposed to be at work right now?"

"Nope. I gave my hours to Mimi," Shay answered, using her cousin to skip the others standing in the long line. It was the first of the month and also the first Friday, which just happened to land on a payday for the working class. Even though Shay had skipped, they still had maybe ten or fifteen people in front of them, and all six of the bank's windows had people being waited on at them.

"Why, so you can go out tonight?"

"Yes and no. Mimi said she needed the extra hours since her boo in jail on a ninety-day probation or some shit like that. His silly ass's really feeling that young-ass nigga to be doing overtime for his ass."

"Shay, stop hating. You need to slow your ass down and find you a man. I'll bet money your ass will be sitting your hot ass down someplace trying to buy a house like the rest of us," Endure said, watching her smile as she quickly responded to a text.

"That shows how much you know. Bitch, I got me a man who likes me just the way I am."

"Who this nigga supposed to be?"

"My baby Slim," Shay said, blushing and all

smiles as she told her how good things were going for her in her new relationship.

~ ~ ~

Danny Boy was the designated driver for the heist that Hood and Ron had planned out for them. As instructed, he dropped them off in front of the bank and made sure he had a clear path to get out of its parking lot without any hassle.

"We finna be in and right outta this bitch. I wish we had one more person to help watch the door and all them muthafuckas in there."

"Ron, fuck that. That's one less nigga we gotta break off a piece of this here easy money. DB, you got this out here, right?" Hood asked while stuffing a duffle bag under his pullover.

"I'm here, ain't I? Fam, you just stay focused on what y'all gotta do, and get in and out like you said." Danny Boy checked his gun. "When I bust in the air, that means get the hell outta there now. Not try and get another dollar. Just come the fuck out!" he said, then watched the two trying to look casual as they got out and approached the entrance. "Lord, if you let me make it away from this mess here today . . . I promise that I'll be in somebody's church this Sunday," prayed Danny Boy, gripping the car's steering wheel nervously.

~ ~ ~

"Is your ass gonna be able to come out with us tonight?" Shay asked after she returned a wink and flirtatious smile with the bank's guard as he passed them for the second time trying to get another view of Endure's big booty in the form-fitting pants she had on.

"Look at you all up in his face. Didn't you just get done telling me about your Mr. Perfect?"

"Hey, I was just teasing him cuz he kept walking

past us looking at that big ole ghetto booty you got back there."

"Bitch, my booty ain't ghetto," Endure chuckled. "I need to get Promiss outta that house cuz she still moping around about Drew. So, yeah. Where y'all trying to go? You know Twista is gonna be at the Onyx. Sharky and Mister finna be up in there, so I ain't gonna be. I need to do me with just my girls tonight," Endure said after reading another text from Sharky on her phone.

Shay lost her words when she saw two masked men with guns enter the bank. The loud boom from the first man's gun got the bank's full attention.

"Now if none of you bitches wanna die in here today, then don't do nothing stupid!" he yelled.

"Get on the fucking floor and throw them cell phones and Bluetooths back my way! All we want is the money and we're gone," the second robber explained to the scared bank tellers while helping his friend strip the two guards of their guns and radios.

Hood roughly pushed the guards to the floor and spotted his gay male cousin, Anthony, on the floor just in front of him and knew he was just the person they needed to help with things.

"Hey you!" He kicked his cousin's leg to get his attention. "Take this fucking bag and get it filled the fuck up!" Hood tossed the bag in his cousin's face when he saw his recognition in his eyes. "The rest of y'all put your faces to the floor!" Ron exclaimed as he went back over to Hood to find out what he was doing making the women get the money. "Man, what's with the bitch?"

"Chill out! That ain't no bitch, that's my cousin Tony. We can trust him to help us. Give me your bag so I can help him while you watch out for us," Hood whispered.

Ron smiled under the mask as he handed him his bag to fill up. He waved his gun back and forth over the people lying on the floor, while covering the two guards with one of the guns that was taken from them.

"This will be over in a second. Don't be dumb. We're not taking your money, just the bank's," Hood explained to everyone as he made his way over to his cousin Anthony. "Hey, cuz. Don't say shit! I already know you know it's me, so just go along with me and I got you!" he promised him in a very low whisper before pressing his jug to his cousin's head and demanding the bank clerk to open the door and let them behind the counter. "Don't try me, or this bitch's brains are gonna be on your mind for the rest of your life!"

The scared little Asian clerk quickly opened the door and was rewarded by Hood's heavy fist in the face and new demands for him to open the small safe that was used to refill the clerks' drawers.

"What the fuck is this shit?" Shay complained in a whisper as she did as she was told. "Why these assholes gotta be doing this shit while we in here?"

Endure didn't answer. She was turned on by the rush of being in a real bank robbery. She had already decided that she was going to get her and her family out of the bank safely. Unknown to Shay, Endure had her gun on her. This was the second time she had felt the need to get out of her truck with her gun on her, because most places don't allow people to walk through the door with them. For the past week she had been having a dream about having to use her gun to save some kids. Now she knew those kids in her dreams were her own that were outside in her truck waiting on her. The need to get out of the bank to them was enough to give her the strength she needed to do something.

"Endure, what you doing? Don't!" she pled when she saw her ease the gun from her purse pocket. "Don't . . . There's two of them. Just let 'em take what they're finna take and go on 'bout their way. Please, girl. I don't want nothing to happen to us."

What Shay didn't know was Endure had been spending a lot of time at the range and was a pretty good shot. With the confidence, she didn't give Shay's pleas any consideration. As soon as her target was where she needed him to be, she would make her move. Endure was just planning to shoot the man covering the door while his buddy was behind the counter and make a run for it with Shay. But then she saw the crossdresser they made help them, walk over to the man at the door, carrying a now full bag, and she had to change her plans.

Anthony was blocking Ron's view as he stood in

front of him waiting for him to tell him what to do next. When Hood came briskly walking from in back, Endure suddenly rolled onto her side and shot him in the chest. She didn't wait to see him hit the floor before she was trading shots with the second bank robber.

Ron was confused and shocked at first but quickly shook it off and exchanged fire with the woman on the floor as she took cover beside a short counter in the middle of the bank's floor.

That gave Endure the opening she needed to get off the shot that ended the gunfight. She was glad for the help because she had used all ten rounds in her .380 Smith and Wesson.

~ ~ ~

Danny Boy heard the gun battle that was suddenly going on inside the bank and quickly pulled the car in front of the door for the getaway just as they planned.

"What the fuck is these niggas doing?" he asked himself aloud with his gun at the ready in his nervous grip. He saw a woman burst out of the bank's doors carrying Hood's red duffle bag and running straight for the car. "Who the hell is you? Where they at?" he asked when Hood's cousin pulled the car door open and tossed the bag inside.

"Whoa, whoa. Help me, I'm hit! She shot me," Anthony said to the gun being held in his face.

"Fuck you!" Danny Boy pulled the trigger, shooting the unknown man in the face. The blast from the big gun knocked Anthony's lifeless body out of the way of the car's door. Once the gunfire had stopped inside the bank, without either of his guys coming out to the car, Danny Boy stomped on the gas pedal, and the car rocketed out of the parking lot, causing the open door to slam shut. As he flew down a few empty, short neighboring blocks, he could hear police sirens in the distance growing ever closer. He turned into an alley, still according to the plan, then nervously rushed and exchanged the car's plates. Danny Boy tossed the old plates into a dumpster then pulled a baby car seat from the trunk along with a few stuffed animals and hastily arranged the items on the backseat and in the rear window of the car before he calmly drove out of the alley and into traffic.

CHAPTER 12

The scene outside the bank was flashing lights everywhere. Heavily armed police officers held back the growing crowd of onlookers that were filling the sidewalks and streets in front of the bank. Black-and-white squad cars were being used as barricades to stop and control the flow of traffic of that portion of North Avenue and the side streets. There were MPD cars, a SWAT truck, and an EMS van parked right out front of the bank's entrance. All of this had started within minutes of the robbery. As soon as all the shooting stopped, the trembling manager along with many of the other frightened employees hastily pressed their panic buttons alerting the police to the robbery.

It was a good thing for Shay and Endure that they had waited so long to call for help, or they would've been gunned down on the spot when they burst out of the bank's doors running to get to the car. When they reached the car, they found the children huddled together down on the floor while crying hysterically. When Endure looked around after Shay had gotten them out of the car, she saw that someone had thrown a jacket over the head of the body lying out in the parking lot, so the children wouldn't have to look at it any more than they had already. The police informed them that they wouldn't be allowed to leave the premises until they were interviewed by the detectives after confiscating Endure's firearm, which was now part of the crime scene.

They placed Shay, Endure, and the kids in one of the bank's offices alone for the wait. While there, they called their family and let them know what had

happened and what was going on.

"Hey, don't say another hot damn word to

nobody until the lawyer gets there. Because even

though you saved the day, them son of a bitches will

find a case to put on you, Endure! So don't say shit

else!" Promiss ordered her. "I'm on. I'll call you back

after I talk to Mike, okay?"

"Yeah, okay. I hear you, but I gotta call Sharky."

"Don't say shit else about what happened, on the

phone or to nobody that's not family, until we get

there. Damn!"

Endure and Shay agreed and let Promiss off the

phone. All they kept repeating to all of their friends

and family members that called or texted them full of

questions, was that they were okay and they would

tell them all about it as soon as they're able. Outside

of the bank all of the television station news crews

were fanned out trying to get the best version of the attempted robbery. Detective Sam Witt and his partner, Gi Lee, were put in charge of the case as soon as their unmarked sedan pulled up and stopped. They were surrounded by news crews and reporters screaming questions at them. Neither detective acknowledged any of them until they were on the other side of the yellow police tape.

"What do we got here?" Witt asked the MPD sergeant who was doing his best to control the chaos going on all around them.

"I got the female shooter and her family waiting for you in the manager's office. I have the rest of the witnesses, which were inside of the bank, over there." The sergeant pointed to a group that stood behind a special taped-off area of the parking lot, giving statements to the police in the area.

"And most of the bank's staff are inside handling

their business. I have statements from the three that were taken to the hospital as well."

"Okay. Thank you. Will you be around if we need a tour guide through all of this?" asked Witt.

"I'm here as long as you need me to be. Just give me a call. I'm on 3B," the sergeant assured them, and then rushed off to aid his men.

"Great." Witt and his partner started toward the bank.

"I'll take the shooter. . . You take the manager. You know the drill; send a text if you need me."

"This is a fucking mess," said Lee, watching the techs pick up a body not far from them before going inside in search of the bank manager. "Are you the manager?" he asked a Ken-doll look-alike.

"Yes. I'm the manager. Name's Kenny Reed."

"I'm Detective Lee, and I know you've given your statement to one of the officers already, but I'm going to need you to please give it to me again. Right now, for you, I'm the most important person that you could be talking to."

"Okay, I understand."

"This will be much easier for the both of us if you show me the video and explain what I can't see."

"Yeah sure. I can access it for in there. Please follow me," the manager said, then led the detective into the corner office and sat down in front of the computer. After his finger danced around the keys, the video he was looking for popped up on the screen.

~ ~ ~

Danny Boy was happy to find that he had the house to himself. He was in no mood for his nosey baby mama who was staying with him until the painters were finished with her place. He knew that right about this time she should be at work and his son was in daycare. Danny Boy's hands were shaking, from the adrenaline that was still rushing through him. This was the first time that a robbery he went on went wrong.

He turned on the television in the front room and turned it to the local news. Danny Boy was the only one who got away, and he wanted to find out if he was the only member of his crew who was still alive. He moved the coffee table away from in front of the sofa to give himself some space, then dumped the money out on the floor. At the same time the breaking news report was starting over. The reporter immediately informed him of the outcome and confirmed his fears.

"In a Milwaukee north side bank, a robbery attempt turned into a deadly shootout inside the bank, leaving four dead and many with minor injuries. . ."

Danny Boy turned the sound up as he sat down

and got busy counting the money that he had made off with.

~ ~ ~

Promiss and a lawyer named Mike Best had arrived on the scene, and while Mike was doing his job in the parking lot with the police, a now very unhappy looking sergeant was ordered to escort the two of them into a makeshift holding cell. It was the same place, the manager's office, that was utilized earlier, and Endure and Shay did as they were told by Promiss and did not give a statement to Detective Witt when he came asking.

Promiss kept her eye on the kids, who were devouring the mini candy bars and cookies that the bank had to offer them. It was a small offering to take their minds off of what they had been witness to less than an hour before. At the same time, Promiss kept peeking through the glass wall of the office at the detective who was trying to busy himself with the bodies that still lie where they had dropped out in the main lobby of the bank. She knew Witt wasn't really doing anything out there but waiting on the lawyer to finish taking the story of Endure and Shay's part in everything so he could have a talk with them.

"All right, ladies, let's get you and these kids outta here. I don't do child law, but I'm sure there is something that forbids keeping small children around something like this here," Mike stated before leading the bunch out of the office.

As soon as the detective spotted the lawyer emerging from the office waving him over to him with the women and children in tow, he rushed over to them.

"What do you think you're doing? I need to speak to these two about what happened here!" Witt confronted him with anger in his voice.

"I'm sorry, but my clients are too upset to give a statement about what happened here over and over to you guys. It's clear that if they hadn't reacted the way they did when they had, this case here would be much harder for you guys, Detective Witt."

"That's not set in stone just yet. My investigation has just started. I'm trying to be nice about this."

"No. You're doing your job; I'm doing mine. Here, this is a recording of the interview I just had with my clients." He handed the detective a small recorder. "I will be needing this back in a few days, so please feel free to make as many copies as you require. Now this is no place for these mothers to have their children, and they are going to get them home now so they can feed them something other than cookies and candy."

"Okay, but make sure they don't leave the city without letting us know first, or I'll be forced to put out a warrant for their arrest," he threatened.

"I'm sure that would go over well with a judge about these heroes that saved the day, Detective Witt."

Shay couldn't help herself. She nonchalantly bent down and retied one of the kid's shoes while sneaking a few stacks of cash for the duffle bag of money that they were standing next to. She hid the money under her shirt in the waistline of her jeans. Then she picked up one of the kids and held him in her arms in order to conceal the now obvious bulge. She calmly followed her lawyer and the detective out of the bank and into their awaiting vehicles.

After watching them drive away, Witt asked his partner, Lee, what he found on the video, because he had a gut feeling he was missing something. Detective Lee told him that all the cameras were in working order and showed a clear story of everything that went on inside and outside of the bank.

"So I can now confirm that at least one of the bank robbers got away with a bag of cash. The video doesn't show his face or the plate number of the sedan that stopped and dropped off two masked men then pulled back up and killed our vic that ran out of the bank to the car. I'm guessing she was trying to ask for help when the driver shot her and took off with the bag of cash."

"That's a he, and maybe he was in on the robbery all along. Get copies of the video ASAP. I want us to go over them from the beginning together. I have a feeling that we will be seeing our heros again soon, and not in a good light."

"What makes you think that? There's nothing in the video that says otherwise."

"If you don't have anything to hide, you don't call a big defense lawyer to come take you home. So, yeah, this is a good day for them, but here's more than meets the eye. I want to know every damn thing about them and the sister who they called that showed up with their lawyer," Witt said, then went over to speak with the others that witnessed the robbery.

CHAPTER 13

Two hundred and eighteen thousand in warm blood money was the total amount that was sitting in front of Danny Boy. The sight of the cash and the realization that it was all his, if he wanted it to be, brought on a whole new rush of adrenaline. The young thug became emotional because his sudden wealth came with such a hefty cost. He hated the loss he felt of the two men he once broke bread with. He sat in a daze, for a moment or two, before he shook off the useless and hurtful thoughts that were trying to steal his joy by making him feel some type of way about being the only one to have survived.

He knew he couldn't do anything for his friends that were now dead, but he could do something to make himself feel better than he did. Danny Boy counted out about $25,000 and then got up and hid the rest of the money that he had stuffed back into the duffle bag, in the dresser in his bedroom. Then he placed $5,500 in an unmarked envelope, and another $6,000 inside a different envelope for his friends.

With a few hours left to be alone before his baby mama and kid made it there, Danny Boy decided to go out and do something nice for them. He stripped out of the clothes he wore for the robbery and then jumped into the shower in the hopes of washing away some of his guilt. About fifteen minutes later he was getting dressed in a black Gucci outfit. Danny Boy gave himself a quick look in the mirror, avoiding making eye contact with himself, then went out to the garage and pulled out his 1979 Cutlass. The car was his pride and joy. He had it painted with royal-blue rally stripes and had twenty-four-inch Dub Floaters, with the name Jack Daniels sewn into the headrest of the soft leather seats. He parked the getaway car in its place just in case anyone saw it and just called it in taking a gamble that it matched the one they were looking for on the news. It's funny how the promise of a grand for information makes some people get, he thought as he pressed play on Drake's hit song "Headlines."

♪*I might be too strung out on compliments*

Overdosed on confidence

Started not to give a fuck and stopped fearing

The consequence

Drinking every night because we drink

To my accomplishments

Faded way too long. I'm floatin' in

And out of consciousness

And they saying I'm back, I agree with that. . . ♪

Danny Boy sang along with the video of Jon dancing and being his old fun self, playing on the car's six television screens as he drove out of the alley behind his place. He turned the radio system up louder, hit repeat on the song by Drake, and headed to deliver the cash-filled envelopes to his fallen friends' homes. His plan was to drop then in their mailboxes without having to explain himself, knowing it was too soon for the family to know of the fate of their loved ones.

Once that was done he took thirty grand over and invested it with his big homie Eshy and MJ, who came up from Chicago and set up shop in the Mil moving heroin like it was running water. Danny Boy knew that if he had parts in the operation, he could make the cash last while he made his exit from living the cold hard street life.

~ ~ ~

"Clear!" the EMT exclaimed loudly, then pressed the two cold pads to her unconscious patient's bare chest and zapped him.

"Nothing! He's still nonresponsive!"

"Again!" the second EMT working on Fame's father ordered.

"Okay. One, two, three, clear!" the first tech repeated the shocking process working hard to restart his heart in the back of an ambulance that was rushing through the streets toward the hospital with a second ambulance racing behind it with the rest of Fame's family inside of it.

~ ~ ~

Fame and Promiss had just arrived at Shay's house for the boxing fight night party that her and Slim had put together to show everyone who cared that they were in a relationship when his phone rang.

"Let me get this. I'll be in when I'm done," he told Promiss when he saw that the call were from his father. Fame knew that for him to be calling him it must be something very important, because texting was Mr. William's preferred way of communication with him over the phone.

"Hurry up. You know the prefight's already started," she reminded him before disappearing inside the house behind Shay and the other.

"What's wrong, Pop?" Fame answered the call.

"Ahlil, this is Queena. Where ya at?"

"Sis, why you calling me off of Pop's phone?

What happened?" he asked his little sister.

"We was in a crash cuz Daddy passed out while he was driving."

"What! Where y'all at?"

"We at St. Michaels Hospital, and you gotta get here, because they won't tell us what's going on with Mama and Daddy. The police just put us in this room and told us not to leave."

"I'm on my way right now. Tell them, if they come back in there, to call me and that I'm on my way there right now, okay?" When she agreed Fame ended then went and found Promiss and Slim.

"Hey, I gotta go. My parents was just in a bad car accident, and the police got my little sister."

"Let's go! I'm coming with you," Promiss told him, putting down the drink she had been sipping.

"Call me and let me know what's going on with

them. I'll be there if you need me to come, bro," Slim assured him while following them out to the car.

Fame raced across the city at fifty miles per hour like it was legal for him to do. When they pulled up in front of the emergency entrance, he left his car double-parked and rushed to the intake desk. There he was pointed toward the hospital room where his mother and two little sisters were.

"Boo, give me your keys so I can go park the car before they have it towed," Promiss said, really only wanting to give Fame a little personal time with everyone.

Fame handed her the keys, and she left the room with his youngest sister by her side. Before they returned, his mother had told him that the accident was because his father suffered a massive heart attack. He was in the midst of making a turn when it happened, so he ended up passing out and crashing into parked cars. The kids were both buckled in while sitting in the backseat, but his mother wasn't. She didn't have her belt on properly because she had to put her shoes back on, and she removed the shoulder strap in order to do so. So when the car came to a hard stop she was thrown into the windshield and knocked unconscious. A few people that witnessed it happen helped get them out of the burning car as well as call 911 for help.

As soon as Promiss and Tahyra returned to the room carrying handfuls of snacks and drinks, the doctor was right behind them with the tragic news that he was unable to revive the husband and father.

CHAPTER 14

Since the death of Fame's father, Promiss noticed
that Fame wasn't himself with her. Whenever she
would call or text him, he was short with her. She
understood that he was trying to grieve and help his
mother plan the funeral at the same time. She didn't
want to lose him and hoped that wasn't what was
happening to their spicy relationship. All of these
thoughts and more ran through her mind as she went
through her closet and pulled out something nice and
plain then got dressed for work. Promiss's plan was
to fill the time she was away from him with work.
Real work, not just sitting in the office giving orders

while she shopped online or chitchatted on social media.

Promiss stood in the mirror and pulled her hair into a ponytail, then smiled at herself before she headed out to the car. She pulled up the song "Please Stay" by Anthony Hamilton, from her playlist, and drove away to work singing along.

♫It's gotten too late and

I've exceeded the moments

To make you stay (Hey baby)

I must've been a fool to run around and not

Once stop to check on you

Hey, baby

Now I've lost my mind and I've given up the time

That I could've shared with you

And if I had my way

I would go down on my knees

And if I had my way

I would go down on my knees

And ask my God to make you stay, Oh. . . ♪

Promiss couldn't help but wonder what Fame was doing, and before she knew it, she sent him a text saying good morning and that she loved him. She smiled big when he replied the same back to her and added that she had a good day at work and that he would talk to her later.

When Promiss arrived at the center, Mimi was the first one through the door to meet her.

"How is Fame doing?"

"He's hurting and trying to do everything on his own."

"Awe. Promiss, if you don't wanna be here and wanna be with your man instead, I'm good to do some overtime. I already talked it over with Endure and Shay. We will just split things up until . . ."

"Mimi, look at me. Don't I look like I'm here to work? Thank you, but I'm good. How my grandma doing?" Promiss asked while walking right into her office.

"She didn't wanna eat this morning, so I didn't make her, but I'ma have to get her to eat something soon cuz she's gotta take her meds," Mimi answered.

"Don't worry about it. I'll take care of her today. She will be happy for me to brush her hair and tell her the latest soap gossip. It works for me every time."

Promiss went to her grandmother's room and found her sitting up in bed staring at a blank television screen. She knew right away that this was one of her bad memory days and the ninety-four-year-old wasn't going to recognize her as family, only another nurse messing with her. Promiss put on her best smile and got to work on making her grandmother feel good enough to take her meds and eat. Anything to keep the thoughts of Fame at bay.

~ ~ ~

Fame wanted to have Promiss at his side but knew she wasn't ready to be inside another funeral home. He loved that she was putting her own grief aside to be there emotionally for him. Now Fame held his mother and sisters as they sat crying at the funeral, staring at his father's polished dark wood coffin that was placed in front of the main altar for all to come and pay their last respects.

When the pastor sang his last song, he called everyone up to say a few words about the deceased. Fame's mother couldn't bring herself to get up from her seat and say goodbye to the love of her life. So

Fame took both of his sisters' hands and went up and spoke for them all. As he finished, he spotted his half-brother, Asad, approaching them from the back of the church.

"Hello, everybody, I'm Asad King. For all of you who don't know me, I have come to pay my last respects to my father and to stand for the King family. I don't have much to say because I didn't allow myself to enjoy my dad's time on this Earth when I was growing up. Now I want him to know I love him and wish I could take it all back and spend every moment with him." Asad then turned to his half-brother. "Bro, it's up to us to be the men our father wanted us to be. We have to be strong for our mother and sisters."

With that said the four of them hugged each other, which made a sad day a little more tolerable.

A wave of cars and trucks along with a large fleet of bikers from the Cobra Motorcycle Club that their father belonged to followed the family limousine as they slowly moved through the streets of the city toward the cemetery. Mr. Earl Williams was laid to rest in a plot beside his mother the way he told them he wanted to be on the day he put her in the ground.

Afterward, most of the family and friends headed over to the repast. Fame and his mother noticed that Ms. King wasn't in attendance of the meal being served in the beautifully decorated hall.

"My mother wanted me to tell you that she's sorry for your loss and that you all will be in her prayers. She didn't mean no kind of disrespect by not being here. She just couldn't get off work," Asad explained to Mrs. Williams and the others.

"Oh, tell her it's none taken and that I understand

and I'm sorry for her loss as well. No, never mind, I'll call her myself. It's about time we sat down and talked like women. Y'all go on over there and get y'all some of that food before it's all gone, now." The mother gave Asad and her children hugs and kisses on the cheeks before allowing herself to get pulled away by one of her husband's good bike buddies.

Queen and Tahyra took to Asad right away. They would not let him get too far away from them. Fame watched his thirteen- and fourteen-year-old sisters smiling and joyously playing with their newly found half-brother. The sight made him feel better about the future.

"Bro, how do you deal with these two?" Asad asked while hiding playfully behind Fame, who was just a few years younger than him.

"I don't know. All they do is hit me up for cash.

That's all their little nappy-head butts want. Money for this and money for that."

The laughing brother had to duck Tahyra's wild right hand as she did her best to slap Fame for saying their hair was nappy.

"Whoa! Whoa! Lil girl, go on somewhere!" Fame told her, laughing.

"Okay, so that's how I can get a break from y'all," Asad said, reaching into his pants pocket.

"No, it's going to be good to have, but we want to know everything about you. So there's no getting rid of us!" Queena spoke up.

Asad handed each of them fifty dollars.

"Okay, I can help you with that, too. See that girl standing over there looking at the photos? Her name is China, and she's my girlfriend, so she can tell y'all all you want to know about me while I talk to your brother."

"Fame is your brother too," Tahyra reminded him after she accepted the money.

When Asad agreed, the girls rushed off to question China about him like he sent them to do, allowing the brothers a few minutes of time to talk to one another.

"I'm telling you now, if you keep that up them two are gonna break you fast."

"It's okay. It's my time to spoil them. Since we're on the subject of money, I want to do my part in helping for things. I don't know how things are for y'all, but he was my dad too, so this falls on all of us."

"Asad, you don't have to do that. But I know I can't stop you, so you're going to have to talk to my mother about it. She won't tell me what she needs help with, so whatever you're planning on doing, I'm telling ya that you're gonna have to put it in her hands," Fame explained to him. "I think she would be cool with that because all she could talk about in the limo was how happy she is that my big brother was here it keep me in line."

"That's good to know, but I think we're going to have to keep each other out of trouble. I won't pull the big brother card on you just yet, but we got to get together in a few days and do some real catching up."

"That sounds good to me, and maybe then my girl will be with me so you can meet her. I didn't invite her to the funeral because she don't handle them all that well, and I didn't want to put her through it just for me," Fame admitted as they walked over to rescue China from the girls.

Mrs. Williams came over to snap pictures of

them all together. She then took Asad off to introduce

him to her curious family and friends who had only

heard of her husband's other son but never seen him

until that day.

CHAPTER 15

Over the next two, closer to three months the brothers spent a lot of time together. They both were curious to know all they could about the man the boys they once knew had become. Fame was amazed by how many of the same people they mingled with and didn't once run into each other over the years. He was also preparing to become an uncle all of a sudden. Asad had two children due in approximately five months by his two beautiful live-in girlfriends.

Fame was getting money in the streets, but nothing like Asad. He had only heard of the amounts and prices of the drugs his brother was playing with, on television or in songs. He never imagined himself on the level of the dope game that he was placed in when he agreed to fill in for Sky and take over the spot once belonging to Zay. Because of all of Fame's new responsibilities, he didn't get to spend much time with Promiss the way she wanted him to. But they made it work by keeping a set date night. China had told them that set date nights was how she got real time with Asad and Sky when they were out in the streets chasing the almighty dollar.

Promiss listened to China, Sky, and Amanda, her three new friends, about making relationships with powerful men work happily. So on her and Fame's date night, she made reservations ahead of time with the manager at Oliver Garden for them and asked to be seated at the same table where Fame had given her the jewelry.

"Baby, this is not the time for you to be checking anything on your phone. It's supposed to be all about us tonight."

"My bad, you're right, but the text was really for you," Fame said, laying the phone face down on the table. "Jasso wants to know if you would want to do business with him and Amanda?"

"What kinda business?"

"That's what I was trying to find out when you made me put the phone down." He flipped his phone over then read the new text. "They want you to let them take over transportation of your people at your job. He said don't say no because Amanda really needs something to do and they got four full-size passenger vans ready to roll right now and he would get more if needed."

"Wow. Tell him okay. We can handle all of that

when it's not our date night," she told him, standing her ground like the others had told her to do on her time with her man. "Fame . . . I got something I really need to say to you, but I need you to promise me that you will hear me out before you say anything."

"Aww, shit!"

"Boo, stop playing. This hard for me enough as it is."

"You don't got nothing to be nervous about, Promiss. You know we can talk about whatever; just say what's on your mind. I won't say shit else until you're done," he promised.

"Okay." She took a couple of slow deep breaths and then stood up and got down on her knee. "I know you're the only one for me because your smile is the key to my heart." She held out an open ring box containing a crushed-diamond, thick, white-gold man's band. "I've tried and tried to talk myself out of loving you, but when I wake up next to you or hear your voice, my whole body and soul reach out for you. So I know my love is here to stay. Fame, please say yes that you'll be my husband?"

Fame was aware that all eyes from the surrounding tables were all on him. He took Promiss's hand and pulled her up on her feet as he stood from his chair.

"Yes! Hell yeah I'll be your husband!" he exclaimed with pride in his voice.

"Let's see it, man!" someone said as Promiss slipped the ring on his finger crying tears of joy in the midst of the onlookers applauding and cheering for them.

Fame slid his hands around the small of her back

and then pulled her close, kissing her long and passionately.

"Let's get out of here. I need some of my soon-to-be wife right now."

"What about our food? I already paid for everything."

"I said now!" he repeated in a low voice, then kissed her again.

Promiss took his hand and allowed him to lead her away from the table. Before leaving the building, she thanked the manager and told him that they wouldn't be eating and that he could have the money as a tip. Then they walked on out to Fame's new black Lincoln Navigator that was sitting on twenty-six-inch shiny black rims. As soon as Fame reached for the back door, Promiss knew he didn't plan on going anyplace soon. She climbed right in the backseat watching his mischievous smile. Fame slid

right between her legs, headfirst, and went to work

on making her cum behind the cover of the night and

the dark tinted windows of the SUV.

CHAPTER 16

Fame stood listening to Byrd explain the details of a job that he had for him and Slim. Once Byrd mentioned Asad's and Zay's name, Fame made his mind up, right there, that he was going to make the hit and would be doing it alone.

"He said the fool-ass nigga's name was Von. Here's the address to a spot he got over on 30th and Michigan and the best picture I could get of his selfie."

"Say, big homie, this one's on me! You sure this was one of Asad's guys he offed, right?" Fame asked, testing to see if Byrd really did not know that him and Asad were brothers. On the outside the only thing to give away that Fame had emotions was the delight in his eyes that he was getting a chance to share the last part of himself with Asad. For weeks he had been trying to find the best way to tell his brother about his life as a hit man for hire.

"Sure as I know my name. Say, if you're not going to take nothing for that nigga, take this to send a message that we ain't to be fucked with!" Byrd told him, pushing some cash into his hand. Byrd had a respectful fear of the young gun for hire, but he wouldn't let him know it.

"Okay, alright. I ain't going to keep turning down no cash. I got baby shit to buy and hair and nails to pay for, just like you niggas. I'm still doing this nigga for free, so this covers the example you want. You'll know when it's done."

"Fo sho!" Byrd agreed, then shook hands with him.

Fame jogged off and disappeared around the corner of the Big Load Laundry Mat leaving Byrd to wonder if he lived in the area somewhere and could move around on foot. The truth was that his new Lincoln wasn't yet known to all, and he wasn't ready to put it out there for it to be. Fame was on the expressway heading toward his new fiancée's place to spend time with her and hopefully convince Promiss into modeling the sexy skimpy lingerie that he bought for her, when his phone began playing Asad's set ringtone.

"What it do, bro?"

"Man, bro man. I just came from hollering at my mans. He told me that he got word on why he killed Zay and shit."

"That's crazy, big bro. I just heard about Zay tonight myself, but it ain't nothing. Is you good though, cuz it sounds like you stressin' on that shit."

"Yeah, a little, cuz I just gotta sit back and trust that whoever the nigga is he put on it will get the job done instead of us going to handle that ourselves. That way I'll know it was done right."

"I feel you, bro, but I'm sure your guy knows that you don't need to be getting your hands dirty. You got too much going on in your life to think about, bro. I gotta good feeling that the situation will be handled the way you need it to be."

"Yeah, you might be right. Where you at? You trying to come fuck with your boy?"

"I was on my way to fuck with Promiss right now, but I can come to you since you got shit on your mind."

"Nawl, I'm good. You go on and kick it with her. I think I'ma go home myself and rub on some feet, and, shit, who knows . . . I might get lucky." Asad chuckled.

"Dude, you got a month or whatever before they have them babies. The state gonna lock your horny ass up for child abuse trying to fuck at a time like they are now."

"See, that's where you're wrong. The doctor told us that it's okay to have sex and that it's good for building a loving relationship between father and child," Asad joked, trying to defend himself.

"I-I-I don't believe no doctor told you no shit like that," Fame said, joining his brother in laughter as he pulled over and parked in front of Promiss's house.

"I hear you getting outta the car, so I take it you made it to her crib. I'ma let you go so you can go in there and make me an uncle. You got some catching up to do."

"Yeah. I'ma pass on that and get some practice in with the two you got on the way before I try to make one of my own."

"You think I meant to do this? I'm still fucked up in the head on how it happened."

"Your ass was fucking without protection is how it happened, nigga. I know better. Promiss on that shot, so I'm good. If you sure you don't want me to come out with you so you can talk, I'ma get off this phone and holla at you later," Fame said when he walked in the house and found Promiss had read his mind and dressed in a white very lacy lingerie set that he had bought her.

"Alright, I'll holla at you on the a.m. Love you, bro," Asad said ending the call.

Fame's thoughts of how Promiss would look on their wedding day would never be the same now that she stood in front of him in all the white lace with yellow flower petals at her feet. He noticed that the petals formed a pathway leading inside the bedroom.

"You got here too fast, but the shocked expression on your face right now works for me also," she said with a naughty grin and lusty gleam in her eyes.

"Damn you look good. Fucking beautiful," he told her while he peeled off his jacket and shoes.

Promiss said nothing, only motioned for him to follow her. Then he walked through the flower pedals and into the candlelit bedroom, making sure that Fame enjoyed the view as she went.

Fame rushed up behind her catching her before she climbed onto the bed. He wrapped Promiss in his arms from behind cupping her thinly covered breasts with his hands and kissing her on her neck. She released a heated moan as she gave in to him. She turned her head so he could press his warm lips to hers. As they kissed, Fame slowly dragged his palms down her body. When he passed her belly button, her knees weekend.

"A-ooh, this is not the way it's supposed to be."

"What's wrong?" he asked, walking kisses down the side of her face.

"I'm supposed to be the one in control right now."

"No . . . You don't. You're gonna be my wife, right?"

"Yesss." The answer was dragged out of her from the feeling he was giving her by running his fingers lightly over the center of the lacy panties.

"Then all of it—everything we do—is about teamwork." He spun her around so they were facing each other. "You push, I pull. You walk, I follow."

"You touch me tender . . . And I cum." She giggled.

"Okay, should I touch you like this?" He bent his head and flicked his tongue on the lace of her bra where her erect nipples were pushing to get free. "Or do you want it like this?" He pulled down the cup and sucked the nipple between his lips.

All she could do was moan in pleasure. Fame's lips were on her skin, and his fingers were now inside her panties. Promiss braced herself on him to keep her knees from giving out. Fame scooped her up and carried her the rest of the way to the bed and placed her gently on it. Promiss grabbed a hold of his shirt and pulled it over his head. As she did so, he pulled away from her. She undid her bra that fastened in the front and let the cups swing loosely as she played with her nipple watching him step out of his pants and boxers. The sight of his hard body and full erection sent a shock through her that made her warmth swell and juice.

As Fame climbed onto the bed with her, he wondered if she would still want him if she knew his dark secrets. And as soon as he was buried deep in her warm wetness, he knew that avenging Zay's murder for his brother would be his last contract killing and prayed she would never find out . . .

CHAPTER 17

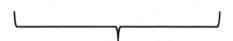

Fame entered the address that he had been given for his target by breaking in through the basement window. He couldn't believe he had been given this hit. He knew it would show his brother that he had real love for him and that they were better together. Fame quickly fell silently inside the window. The basement was dark, wet, and filled with junk. He walked up the stairs, two at a time, and put his ear to the door to listen for any movement before making another move. When he didn't hear anything, he eased open the door while being cautious not to make a noise.

He crept through the grimy and dimly lit house unnoticed. He saw dope heads passed out in almost every filthy corner of the spot. Some of them had needless hanging out of their arms and legs or wherever else they could inject the powerful drug into their system. This was good for Fame because none of them paid him any mind as he moved past them. He came up on one of the workers sitting with his back toward him.

The guy was deep into a game that he was playing on his cell phone. Fame slipped his blade from his pocket, then quickly slit the man's throat with the same knife he used to pry open the basement window. He picked up the dead man's gun that was lying on the table and looked at his face to see if he had gotten lucky and killed Von on the first try. But he was not the person he came for, so he continued moving about the shadows throughout the house.

Soon, the focused executioner came to another set of stairs just outside of the trash-littered dining room. The stairs led up to the second floor where he could hear music. Fame hoped that's where he would find his target as he climbed the steps two at a time with his back to the wall. He moved swiftly, so he kept close to the wall for his own good. A door just behind his suddenly opened, and when he turned toward it, he saw Von emerge from the room adjusting his belt after using the toilet.

As soon as Von seen Fame's unfamiliar face, he went for his gun, knowing that none of their junkies were allowed on the floor of the house without an escort.

"Hey! What the fuck are you doing up here?"

Fame already had the gun he had taken from the

table on the first floor, in his hand.

"I was looking for you!" Fame answered as he quickly raised the gun and squeezed the trigger getting his shot off first. His shots hit Von in his chest.

The big hot slugs spun Von around like a spin toy as Fame sent a few more shots through his back and side before Von's body hit the floor. The bloodthirsty goon then stood over the dying man's body and emptied the rest of the clip into his head.

All of the gunfire brought the rest of the house workers out. MJ was getting some head from one of the pretty dope-head females when he heard the shots over the pounding music playing in the room he was in. He roughly pushed the women out of his way, pulled up his Dickies, grabbed his gun, and ran from the room to investigate what was going on.

MJ unexpectedly found himself witness to the savage murder of one of his best friends at the hands of the stone-faced killer. Without saying a word, after making sudden eye contact, they immediately began exchanging gunfire. Fame had to dive from the bathroom's doorway to the stairs so he wouldn't be trapped by MJ's rapid, wild gunshots. MJ ran after him, which caused Fame to slip and fall over the banister. A dirty couch broke his fall, but he didn't waste time counting his blessings. He rolled to his feet just in time to dodge the shots that ripped through what was left of the fake leather pillows on the couch.

Another one of the young goons rushed to the aid of his boss only to be killed before he could ever prove his worth. Fame made his way to the front door, and as soon as he stepped through the exit, he saw a scarred man who was standing just off the side

of it. Fame gunned him down just in case he found

the courage to use the gun in his hand. A junkie tried

to grab him as he ran, but Fame easily slipped out of

his loose grasp. Now off the porch, Fam ran as fast

as he could while trying to reach one of the two

stolen cars that he had placed at opposite ends of the

block for his getaway.

He made it just in time to witness the first of

many MPD squad cars hitting the block. They were

obviously responding to a flood of 911 calls made by

the neighbors once they heard all of the shots being

fired inside the house. He took a few calming breaths

then pulled out his phone and called Byrd.

"It's done but not over. There's a lesson still to

be taught that you paid for, and it will be given. Just

keep watching for it," Fame said, then chuckled at

what he had just gone through.

"Okay! Go chill out for the night. My nigga wants to meet you to thank you himself. He's good people."

"I know. I'll get up with him in a minute, but right now I'm gone." With that said he ended the call. Fame thought of how Von had just lost his life trying to impress a female.

"Who says money is the root of all evil? Pussy is a cold bitch." He laughed aloud then turned on the radio and sang along with MJ as the local radio station played his hit song "Reckless," in the nightly hot mix.

~ ~ ~

Danny Boy and Eshy were just pulling up on the block, confused by all the chaos and police lights. They were just about to start making a call, when MJ suddenly appeared from a gangway where he had been running through in his escape from the spot.

"Fam! Over here!" Danny Boy yelled to him from the car window.

"Aye, follow that wagon right there!" MJ said as soon as he was inside. "He just ran in our spot and got all that shit started," he explained, pointing to the light blue Chevy station wagon that sat parked on the corner.

"Who the fuck is that?" Eshy asked as Danny Boy took off toward the wagon.

"I don't know! Who got another burner? Mine's empty."

"Here." Danny Boy passed MJ his gun so he could help Eshy try to stop the wagon, since he had to drive.

~ ~ ~

As soon as Fame put the wagon in gear to pull away, the rear window imploded suddenly. He instantaneously stomped the accelerator then chanced looking in the rearview mirror while zigzagging in and out of busy 27th Street traffic. He couldn't see who was back there shooting at him, but he guessed that they were more guys from the dope house. When he reached Vliet Street, he made a hard left blasting right through the stoplight. They were still on him, so he made another desperate turn onto 29th Street racing north with Danny Boy hot on his tail.

They blew through the stop sign, on 30th and Cherry, and Danny Boy's car was T-boned by a speeding firetruck that sent them sailing into the apartment building on the corner. The loud crash made Fame look back to see what had happened. He was about to laugh when he slammed into a small SUV that had suddenly backed out of a driveway. Conscious, but dizzy, he slid out the window of the wagon and abruptly took off toward Vliet Street.

Eshy was instantly killed by the collision with the big speeding firetruck, but Danny Boy and MJ escaped with only cuts and bruises. They ran from the scene refusing treatment from the skilled lead of the first responders. Danny Boy turned into an alley with MJ right behind him. Once there, they stopped to rest and discuss their best next move.

Fame had a big gash over his eye that was leaking blood down his face, so he cut through a nearby gangway to get off the main streets knowing the police would be out looking for anyone with his description and in his condition. He still had his gun and phone. Fame's plan was to get someplace where he could rest and hide and call Slim to come get him. But as he stepped foot in the alleyway, he found himself face-to-face with the men he had been running from.

Without hesitation, MJ and Fame simultaneously raised their guns and exchanged fire. Danny Boy dived behind a row of plastic recycle bins because he was unarmed and there was no place else to go. Fame's shot killed MJ, hitting him directly in the heart. MJ's shot hit Fame in the thigh and hip sending him crashing to the ground where he lost grip of his gun. He also hit his head hard enough to knock him unconscious.

All of the gunfire led the police right to them. Danny Boy stayed down when the black-and-white drove past him then stopped just short of where the two bodies were lying. When the two officers got out with their guns at the ready and focused on them, Danny Boy used the time to hop the gate he was closest to and walked away. He was happy that he still had his life and planned on leaving the city for someplace smaller were he could start over.

Fame awoke in cuffs, being put in the back of an ambulance to be taken to the hospital, and he knew without a doubt from there to jail for the man he had killed that was still lying on the cold alley floor.

"Somebody help me please. They're trying to kill me!" Fame shouted out loud enough for the policewoman who was escorting him to the hospital to hear, then allowed himself to pass out again.

CHAPTER 18

Detective Kare was sitting at her desk at work searching for information on the second female's identification card that she had been given by the girlfriend of Mercy Bondz's son when she received the call about another multiple homicide. Since she hadn't been assigned a new partner yet, it was all on her to go investigate. She quickly left the station and drove to the scene of a witness-reported shootout inside a house on 30th and Michigan Avenue.

When she arrived on the scene there was a fleet of MPD black-and-white squad cars along with a few other of the city's emergency vehicles parked every which way, all crowded in front of the house. Kare wedged her car in where she could then got out with the last of her iced coffee in her hand. She downed it then took a few deep calming breaths before making her way over to the house.

The detective dropped her empty plastic drink in the trash bin at the curb then walked up onto the porch. There she found a light-complexioned male with most of his lower jaw gone from an obvious close-range shot to his face.

"Excuse me?" Kare said, flashing her gold shield. "What all do we have on our hands here?" she quizzed one of the two uniformed officers that was having a conversation while standing next to the body.

"It's a mess, Detective, is all I can tell you," he answered, turning to face her. "Besides that poor fella there, there's a few more inside." He pointed at the wide-open front door of the house. "I really don't know much else because we've been ordered to stand out here and keep the nosey reporters away, and I'm good with that."

"I know how you feel. No matter how many you see of this kinda thing, it never gets any easier to see. I don't want to be here right now myself, I had forty-five minutes to go before I could punch the clock when this call came in. But it's the job I signed up for," she said as she stepped over to the body lying on the floor of the dirty porch.

Kare was down attentively viewing the body of the murdered thug when another uniformed officer walked over to her.

"Excuse me, are you Detective Kare?" the female officer inquired.

"Yes. Why?" Kare answered, looking up from the corpse.

"They need you inside."

"What do they have in there that can't wait until I'm done here?" she asked, shaking her head at the rookie who was getting paler by the second. "Please don't puke all over my crime scene. If you gotta, go over to the curb."

"I'm good." She stood up tall. "It's another male vic. I found him, but unlike that guy, this one's throat has been slashed."

"Okay. If you're good, lead the way." Detective Kare clicked off her flashlight and followed the officer inside. She immediately clicked it back on when she stepped inside of the gloomy dilapidated interior. It smelled like gun powder and something sour and very strong. Kare was taken to a body slumped awkwardly in a chair that was almost decapitated beside a dirty table. "Did you find any weapons on him?" she asked, leaning in closer, skimming the beam of her flashlight up and down the victim.

"Weapons?"

"Yes, weapons. The guy on the porch still had his finger on the trigger, and from the look of this place it was a drug house, so I'm sure this guy also has a gun on him."

"I didn't touch the body, but looked all around and didn't see one."

"Alright. Get the team up in there and tell them to photograph every inch of this room before anything is moved. I'm going to check out the bodies upstairs if you need me," the detective said, walking over to the staircase. The first thing she observed was the broken banister and the bullet-riddled sofa beneath it. She knew that someone had either fallen or jumped down from the second floor. "Hey, you, tell them to also get shots of all of this area too please?" she exclaimed, then continued up the flight of stairs where she came right up on the third body in the house so far. From what she could see, there was no need for the body shots, and if they came first, then there wasn't a reason for the face shot, unless this murder was personal.

"Hey, Detective Kare!" the first uniformed officer from the porch called to her from the middle of the staircase.

"Yeah?" she answered, walking back to the top of the stairs.

"I just got word that they caught the suspect from here. He's on his way to the hospital from being T-boned by a speeding firetruck," he explained excitedly.

"That's good to know. Find out where he's being taken for me. I'll come find you when I'm done up here," she told him, then went back to work investigating. She hoped the two really were connected so she could get this case closed and get back to the Bondz murder.

~ ~ ~

The continuous reverberation of Asad's phone woke up China, while he just shifted to a new spot and kept snoring. She glanced at the time on the clock and guessed that it must be very important. So, still half asleep, she reached over him and snatched up the ringing cell phone.

"Hello? There better be a real damn emergency call this early."

"This is Byrd. I need to talk to Asad."

"Byrd, he's sleeping. What's wrong?"

"Wake him up. He needs to go to the hospital because Fame got shot."

"Oh God, is he alright? Hold on." She shook Asad awake. "Here, it's Byrd. He said your brother got shot," she explained while clumsily passing him the phone.

"What?" Asad snapped awake, snatching the phone out of her hand. "What the fuck happened?" he demanded frantically as he sat up in bed.

"Brenda just called and told me Fame was brought through the emergency room by the police about a half hour ago. She said he got shot and is fucked up really bad, bro, so you need to get over there," Byrd explained.

Asad ended the call and rolled out of bed to get

to his brother. Both he and China rushed around the room, quickly dressing to leave.

"Boo. I know you're in a hurry, but slow down. It won't do any of us any good if you get hurt."

"I'm good. I just need to find out what the fuck he was doing to be shot by the police and what his ass was doing out so late anyway. This shit's crazy," Asad responded, then tossed on some gray sweatpants, socks, and shoes. "China, get up with Sky and make sure she good. I'ma call you when I find out what's up with Fame," he told her, then raced out of the house.

Asad sped through the streets. He had been out of the house less than ten minutes when his phone rang, and this time it was Sky calling to let him know that she was alright and she would meet him up at the hospital. Another ten minutes passed, and he was turning onto the grounds of the hospital. Asad found a parking spot and slid his car in it then jumped out and frantically jogged through the emergency room's entrance and up to the information desk. He demanded to be pointed in the direction of his brother.

"He was shot by the police and brought here like an hour ago. So what do you mean you don't know anyone here that's been shot by the police?"

"Sir, I've been here all night. It's my job to know who is in the ER, and I'm telling you, someone gave you the wrong information. But if you calm down and give me his name again, I can look him up and see if he is here for a different reason for you, okay?" the night nurse explained. "Sir, your brother is here. He was shot but not by the police. He's in critical condition right now is all I can say at this time."

"What room is he in?"

"I can't give you that information, but if you have a seat in the waiting area, I'll call someone to come speak with you to answer that question."

"Alright," Asad agreed, then went and sat down in a seat that gave him the best view of the front desk and the emergency doors. While he waited, he texted Byrd and asked him to call Brenda and tell her that he was in the waiting room. A few minutes later she emerged through the double doors.

"Hey, do you know what's going on, because old girl won't tell me shit."

"Asad, I don't know much. The police won't let many people around him, but I do know that he was shot and in a bad car accident with a firetruck. The doctors are working on him as hard as they can to stop the bleeding right now. Once they get him stable, I'll know more and come get you," Brenda told him, then rushed back off through the double doors leaving him to wait some more.

Asad turned his attention to the television and saw a special breaking news report. What caught his attention most was when they talked about a high-speed chase that ended with a car being T-boned by a firetruck.

EPILOGUE

When Promiss couldn't reach Fame by phone call or text, she got worried and decided to go over to his house. It was unlike him not to return her calls and texts or not be in bed beside her. As she drove, she wondered if Fame was changing his mind about them, but then pushed the thought out of her mind. Things had been going too well between them for him to have a change of heart. Her final thought as she parked in front of his house was that Fame had just fallen asleep and wasn't hearing his phone, which she knew was almost always kept on vibrate.

Promiss got out of the car and rang his
doorbell a few times. As she waited on an answer,
she looked over the edge of the porch and glanced in
the back to see if his car was there. It wasn't. She
tried Fame's phone again while this time banging on
his front door. Still no answer. Now she was worried
all over again. She got back in her car to head over to
his mother's house when her phone rang. Promiss
looked at the screen and saw it was an unknown
number calling.

"Hello?" Promiss answered while starting her
car.

"Is this Promiss?" asked a female voice.

"Yes, who is this?"

"I'm a nurse at Mount Sinai Hospital. I see you're

trying to reach one of our John Does. Could you please tell me the name of the man you were just trying to call, so we can better help him?"

"Oh my God, no! Is he. . .? He—" Promiss couldn't ask the question.

"No ma'am. He's alive. We just don't have a name, so we call him John Doe," the nurse explained. "I'm sorry about that!"

"Thank you! His name his Famous Williams. What is he there for?"

"I'm sorry, I am unable to say over the phone. Mr. Williams is in critical condition, and we have him in our intensive care unit. He was admitted earlier this morning, and this was the first time we've had time to contact family for him."

"I'm on my way there. I'ma pick up his mother, and we'll be right there," Promiss said, ending the call. Then she immediately called Fame's mother to tell her what was going on with her son and that she was on her way to pick her up, so they could go to the hospital together.

To Be Continued

To order books, please fill out the order form below:
To order films please go to www.good2gofilms.com

Name:_____ Address:_____ City:____State:____Zip Code: _
Phone:_____ Email:_____ Method of Payment: Check VISA MASTERCARD
Credit Card#:_ ____ Name as it appears on card: ____ Signature: ____

Item Name	Price	Qty	Amount
48 Hours to Die – Silk White	$14.99		
A Hustler's Dream - Ernest Morris	$14.99		
A Hustler's Dream 2 - Ernest Morris	$14.99		
A Thug's Devotion – J. L. Rose and J. M. McMillon	$14.99		
All Eyes on Tommy Gunz – Warren Holloway	$14.99		
Affliction 1 - Assa Raymond Baker	$14.99		
Affliction 2 - Assa Raymond Baker	$14.99		
Black Reign – Ernest Morris	$14.99		
Bloody Mayhem Down South – Trayvon Jackson	$14.99		
Bloody Mayhem Down South 2 – Trayvon Jackson	$14.99		
Business Is Business – Silk White	$14.99		
Business Is Business 2 – Silk White	$14.99		
Business Is Business 3 – Silk White	$14.99		
Cash In Cash Out – Assa Raymond Baker	$14.99		
Cash In Cash Out 2 - Assa Raymond Baker	$14.99		
Childhood Sweethearts – Jacob Spears	$14.99		
Childhood Sweethearts 2 – Jacob Spears	$14.99		
Childhood Sweethearts 3 - Jacob Spears	$14.99		
Childhood Sweethearts 4 - Jacob Spears	$14.99		
Connected To The Plug – Dwan Marquis Williams	$14.99		
Connected To The Plug 2 – Dwan Marquis Williams	$14.99		
Connected To The Plug 3 – Dwan Williams	$14.99		
Cost of Betrayal – W.C. Holloway	$14.99		
Cost of Betrayal 2 – W.C. Holloway	$14.99		
Deadly Reunion – Ernest Morris	$14.99		
Dream's Life – Assa Raymond Baker	$14.99		
Flipping Numbers – Ernest Morris	$14.99		

Flipping Numbers 2 – Ernest Morris	$14.99		
He Loves Me, He Loves You Not - Mychea	$14.99		
He Loves Me, He Loves You Not 2 - Mychea	$14.99		
He Loves Me, He Loves You Not 3 - Mychea	$14.99		
He Loves Me, He Loves You Not 4 – Mychea	$14.99		
He Loves Me, He Loves You Not 5 – Mychea	$14.99		
Killing Signs – Ernest Morris	$14.99		
Killing Signs 2 – Ernest Morris	$14.99		
Kings of the Block – Dwan Willams	$14.99		
Kings of the Block 2 – Dwan Willams	$14.99		
Lord of My Land – Jay Morrison	$14.99		
Lost and Turned Out – Ernest Morris	$14.99		
Love & Dedication – W.C. Holloway	$14.99		
Love Hates Violence – De'Wayne Maris	$14.99		
Love Hates Violence 2 – De'Wayne Maris	$14.99		
Love Hates Violence 3 – De'Wayne Maris	$14.99		
Love Hates Violence 4 – De'Wayne Maris	$14.99		
Married To Da Streets – Silk White	$14.99		
M.E.R.C. - Make Every Rep Count Health and Fitness	$14.99		
Mercenary In Love – J.L. Rose & J.L. Turner	$14.99		
Money Make Me Cum – Ernest Morris	$14.99		
My Besties – Asia Hill	$14.99		
My Besties 2 – Asia Hill	$14.99		
My Besties 3 – Asia Hill	$14.99		
My Besties 4 – Asia Hill	$14.99		
My Boyfriend's Wife - Mychea	$14.99		
My Boyfriend's Wife 2 – Mychea	$14.99		
My Brothers Envy – J. L. Rose	$14.99		
My Brothers Envy 2 – J. L. Rose	$14.99		
Naughty Housewives – Ernest Morris	$14.99		
Naughty Housewives 2 – Ernest Morris	$14.99		
Naughty Housewives 3 – Ernest Morris	$14.99		
Naughty Housewives 4 – Ernest Morris	$14.99		
Never Be The Same – Silk White	$14.99		
Scarred Faces – Assa Raymond Baker	$14.99		

Scarred Knuckles – Assa Raymond Baker	$14.99		
Shades of Revenge – Assa Raymond Baker	$14.99		
Slumped – Jason Brent	$14.99		
Someone's Gonna Get It – Mychea	$14.99		
Stranded – Silk White	$14.99		
Supreme & Justice – Ernest Morris	$14.99		
Supreme & Justice 2 – Ernest Morris	$14.99		
Supreme & Justice 3 – Ernest Morris	$14.99		
Tears of a Hustler - Silk White	$14.99		
Tears of a Hustler 2 - Silk White	$14.99		
Tears of a Hustler 3 - Silk White	$14.99		
Tears of a Hustler 4- Silk White	$14.99		
Tears of a Hustler 5 – Silk White	$14.99		
Tears of a Hustler 6 – Silk White	$14.99		
The Last Love Letter – Warren Holloway	$14.99		
The Last Love Letter 2 – Warren Holloway	$14.99		
The Panty Ripper - Reality Way	$14.99		
The Panty Ripper 3 – Reality Way	$14.99		
The Solution – Jay Morrison	$14.99		
The Teflon Queen – Silk White	$14.99		
The Teflon Queen 2 – Silk White	$14.99		
The Teflon Queen 3 – Silk White	$14.99		
The Teflon Queen 4 – Silk White	$14.99		
The Teflon Queen 5 – Silk White	$14.99		
The Teflon Queen 6 - Silk White	$14.99		
The Vacation – Silk White	$14.99		
Tied To A Boss - J.L. Rose	$14.99		
Tied To A Boss 2 - J.L. Rose	$14.99		
Tied To A Boss 3 - J.L. Rose	$14.99		
Tied To A Boss 4 - J.L. Rose	$14.99		
Tied To A Boss 5 - J.L. Rose	$14.99		
Time Is Money - Silk White	$14.99		
Tomorrow's Not Promised – Robert Torres	$14.99		
Tomorrow's Not Promised 2 – Robert Torres	$14.99		
Two Mask One Heart – Jacob Spears and Trayvon Jackson	$14.99		
Two Mask One Heart 2 – Jacob Spears and Trayvon Jackson	$14.99		

Two Mask One Heart 3 – Jacob Spears and Trayvon Jackson	$14.99		
Wrong Place Wrong Time – Silk White	$14.99		
Young Goonz – Reality Way	$14.99		
Subtotal:			
Tax:			
Shipping (Free) U.S. Media Mail:			
Total:			

Make Checks Payable To: Good2Go Publishing, 7311 W Glass Lane, Laveen, AZ 85339